Dressed
up as
Love

BY LOLO STUBBS

Bronzite Books Publishing
Colony
5 Piccadilly Place
Manchester
M1 3BR

www.bronzitebooks.co.uk/
info@bronzitebooks.co.uk

CONTENTS

CHAPTER 1.

LOST

As the credits at the end of the film began to roll and the title music blasted from the television, Melissa jerked out of her daydream, back into reality. In yet another half-cut state, she stared at the empty bottle of Merlot, the melted remains of half a tub of cookie dough ice cream and a packet of cigarettes, that were strewn across the couch where she lay. She was alone in her living room - yet again, in the house she was supposed to share with her partner Chris - Chris Clancy, however, all she ever seemed to have for company were those same four walls. She reached out for her cigarettes, wondering just when and how she had become a full-time smoker. She lit up and inhaled deeply. For that second, she felt a little better, her nerves a little less fraught, but then, as she replayed the evening's events back in her mind, one lonely, isolated tear grazed her cheek and a vacant expression returned to her face. His words were cutting like a knife all over again. She hoisted herself up from the couch and with a slight stumble, she made her way over to the fireplace - looking into the large pine-framed mirror above it, she stared at herself. Her face appeared emotionless, almost lifeless behind her tear-glazed eyes. Her brows furrowed slightly, as a whirlwind of thoughts began to run through her head; 'yet another night on my own?'; 'yet another night drunk?'.

She drank pretty much every night to numb the pain, consuming cigarette after cigarette, trying to fill the void she felt inside. In an attempt to focus her eyes, she blinked away her tears. Her face was puffy, red and swollen, having spent the last couple of hours sobbing. Wondering how it was even possible that she had any tears left to cry, she took another prolonged drag on her cigarette. She exhaled and watched as the curtain of smoke covered her reflection. As the smoke dispersed, she continued to glare at her own eyes; they had always been icy blue in colour, but now all she seemed to see in them was grey, and she felt like she was looking at somebody else. It was like she had become a stranger in her own body, and she didn't recognise herself anymore.

Tonight, had been much the same as any other night, beginning with Chris returning home from work (hours later than he said he would), the dinner she slaved over being ruined and consequently, he would start hurling around harsh insults in Melissa's direction - Chris needed very little excuse to put her down and criticise her. She would try and reason with him, asking him why he kept being that way with her - so dismissive of her feelings; usually, it led to her sobbing and begging to understand what exactly it was that she had done wrong? It wouldn't be long before he would storm out of the house, after firing out a tirade of humiliating blows, leaving her wounded, distraught and very often dropping to the floor with emotional exhaustion. He wouldn't return until the early hours of the morning. This daily ritual was like living in 'Groundhog Day', 'week' and even 'month'.

The argument (just like all the others) had been yet another dent in her self-esteem - that is, if she had any self-esteem left to dent. Night after night, she desperately tried to distract herself from the invasion of loneliness that would creep in. Melissa was unaware that she has been firmly locked in an abusive relationship for the past 3 years, cleverly administered on a subtle drip feed - one that left her so tormented that when he so frequently said, 'There's something seriously wrong with you!', 'Your paranoid - it's all in your head', it did indeed leave her questioning her own mentality.

'*Am I ill*? Is it *me*?'

She would often stare in the mirror as if she was asking a different person, and then the repetitive, insane questioning within her own mind would begin.

This was, of course, all part of the disturbing mind games that saw a bright young girl totally diminish in character. Her light had previously shone so bright and everywhere she went everyone noticed her. Whilst Melissa may have been totally oblivious of her natural charisma and ability to attract the attention of a whole room, Chris had always been *more* than aware of her magnetic qualities - it was, after all, such qualities that attracted him to her in the first place. Sadly, his paranoia that someone else would fall for her in the same way he had, and want to steal her away from him, meant that he made sure that, year upon year, her light gradually dimmed, watching without remorse, as she slipped away into a shadow of her former self.

Melissa's nature was warm, sincere, and fun-loving (it still is) but when they first met, she had a real feistiness about her; in fact, she was quite the feminist at heart. She certainly wasn't one to be told what to do by anyone - let alone a boyfriend - so at the start of their relationship they were very much on equal terms. It was only when she returned from that fateful girly holiday to Cyprus that things began to change. That feisty side of her had disappeared; she had come home a different person, secretly harbouring deep wounds and demons, that over the years would only become more deep-rooted and painful as she tried without success to bury them.

'Do you realise how lucky you are to have me?', she could hear his arrogant statement echoing around her head. He would blast those same words at her day after day, week after week, month after month and had done so increasingly for at least the past 3 years. She felt so low and so ashamed when she returned from *that* 'holiday' that she believed him and with every word, each day, more of her confidence slipped away. Chris became a real Jekyll and Hyde character, thereafter, taking advantage of her new 'pushover' persona. However, for the past year, she had only really seen the 'Hyde side' and something inside her was beginning to stir - something was changing. This wasn't just another drunken daydream for a much longed-for state of independence, it was her old self awakening, fighting to come back to life. 'Look at yourself'; 'Look at what you have allowed him to do to you'; she glared at the reflection in the mirror, an anger rousing within her gut. She didn't even know where to begin in order to find herself again, but with a look of determination, she wiped away the tears that were streaming down her blotchy cheeks, inhaled deeply and nodded to herself reassuringly. "This has got to stop! You can't keep living like this!"

she cried out, as she shouted at her herself, "For God's sake, Melissa, what's happened to you?", sobbing even further, the fact she was shouting at herself in the third person only highlighted her sense of insanity and how little she could see herself in her own reflection. Tears streamed down her cheeks, in a constant river-like fashion. "Shit! Ouch!" she yelped as the cigarette burnt her fingers and she dropped it to the floor. It had burnt all the way down; there was a mound of ash on the floor below along with the cigarette dimp that was still burning, after she became lost in a whirl of thoughts and emotions. "Shit, Shit!" She quickly stooped down, panicking, and accidentally stubbed out the cig in the half-eaten ice cream tub and not the ashtray. She started to stumble into the kitchen to get a cloth to clean up when she noticed her phone on the side. It would be pointless to check it, as she wouldn't hear or see from Chris until at least the early hours of the morning. Telling herself she wasn't bothered anyway, she still reached for it to check. She often spoke to herself, every evening in fact – well, there wasn't anyone else to talk to! Melissa had lots of lovely family and friends, but they were blissfully

7

unaware of the torment she was secretly enduring and she, therefore, locked herself away most nights, alone with only her own thoughts and his brutal insults swirling around her head. She did get a kitten for company, but that didn't quite work out as all she ended up with was a mass of scratches and feeling more trapped than ever - quite literally in fact, as she was too afraid to leave the bedroom!

YOU HAVE 1 NEW MESSAGE FROM ANTHONY – R U awake? Wondered if I could call round?

'That's strange', she thought, looking puzzled as she studied the text, squinting her eyes as she tried to alleviate the alcohol-induced double vision.

Anthony was in a relationship with Chris's sister, Louisa. Melissa had been friends, or rather acquaintances with Louisa originally, as she knew her from school, but as they had gotten older, Louisa - like Chris, had become increasingly arrogant and Melissa only tolerated her company when she had to. Louisa had been dating Anthony for around the same length of time that she and Chris had. Although Anthony and Louisa didn't officially live together yet, he spent most of his nights staying over there. Melissa didn't think very highly of Anthony since they had fallen out around two years ago. Before that, they had always been fairly close. She had always enjoyed his company back when they all started dating, clubbing, and generally embracing their early adult life together. A large group of them would all go out and holiday together. However, whilst they were all away for the weekend in Spain, things took an unexpected turn during their second night out there. Out of the blue, Chris ripped Melissa's purse and keys from her during a very public dressing-down, in the middle of a beachfront bar. Chris's sudden eruption towards her made no sense at all and left her completely bewildered. It happened, (according to Chris) after Anthony had allegedly informed him of her behaving in a way that he didn't approve of. Melissa had no idea what it could have been, as she had simply walked from one bar to another along with the rest of the group. The event consequently led to her spending the night alone, humiliated and scared on the beach, as Chris had stormed out of the bar, taking her keys and purse with him. She never did confront Anthony; she didn't dare, and she never did know exactly what had been said or what she was supposed to have done. She just didn't trust Ant anymore though and no longer wanted to be his friend- she also decided holidays were not for her, after two dreadful experiences!

After Melissa and Chris moved in together, both Chris and Louisa forced her to reconcile with Anthony, as her stubbornness towards the situation did not bode well with their need for a seemingly picture-perfect family appearance, to portray to the outside world. ('The Clancy's were a well-to-do family and were very much about keeping up with the Jones's and portraying the perfect family life.)

Maybe it was because she was drunk, maybe it was because she so desperately needed the company, who knows, but she picked up the phone and called Anthony.

"Hello," Anthony answered rather chirpily.

"Hiya, I'm sorry, I've only just seen your text," she slurred slightly, apologising after she realised that he had sent it an hour ago. "I won't be great company, but, if you still want to, if it's not too late now, you can come around if you want to?" she repeated.

"Yes, of course! I'm just finishing fixing the headlight on my car. I'll be done in about 20 mins, Louisa is in town until later and I've got to wait up to pick her up, so it's not too late, it's fine."

"Oh, ok, I'll see you in a bit, then."

"See you later!"

As the phone cut off, she pondered, why the sudden 'let's be friends' act? Chris and Louisa weren't around to witness it, so it wasn't like he was going to get any brownie points off them for it, so she couldn't understand why he was calling. However, she had always been one to give people the benefit of the doubt, so she decided it was wrong of her to doubt whether he was being genuine, after all the past was the past, and 'we were all younger then,' she thought. And besides, she never did have it out with Anthony as to why he had caused the trouble between her and Chris, perhaps it was a misunderstanding, *perhaps* it was Chris making things up all along? She wouldn't put anything past

11

Chris now that she was finally starting to see the light!

She continued to ponder over the various questions that were popping into her thoughts, when it suddenly dawned on her that she was stood in the middle of her lounge - looking rather worse for wear - not to mention the fact the house could do with a quick tidy to hide any evidence that she had been drowning her sorrows. Melissa was always one to put a smile on and hide her feelings behind it - no matter what, and she didn't want Anthony, or anyone for that matter, to see her this fragile. She dashed around the living room, collecting up the empty wine bottle, wine glass and ice cream tub, she kicked the ash that was scattered on the floor and the ashtray underneath the settee, as she couldn't carry anything else. She quickly ran upstairs, bouncing off the wall at least once along the way. She shoved the items on to the top of the drawers in the darkened spare room and then dashed to the bathroom. She switched on the light; the brightness of the light reflecting off the white walls took her aback momentarily, and she began splashing her face with cold running water. As she looked into the bathroom mirror with the cool water dripping from her face, she realised it would take more than a splash of cold water to soothe her face and hide the fact that she had spent the last two hours or so crying.

DING – DONG

"Oh shit!" she said aloud, "that wasn't 20 minutes!" She had no time to disguise her pain; her mask had slipped, and she was about to be caught out, but what should she do? She thought briefly about what excuse she could use as to why she would have been upset and then realised she was all out of excuses. She had covered up for Chris and their shambles of a relationship far too many times and she was completely exhausted by doing so. 'Why am I still protecting him?', she questioned; suddenly she seemed to stop caring. She got to the bottom of the stairs that led directly into the lounge and headed towards the front door, taking in a deep breath as she pushed down the handle and opened it.

"Alright, Zippy!" (Anthony had always playfully called Melissa that back when they were friends). It caught her off guard a little, as she hadn't heard him refer to her like that in so long. She smiled, not only with her mouth, but a little with her eyes and she strangely felt a little more alive.

Melissa had a big smile - hence the reference to Zippy - and it could light up a room. Her naturally curly brunette hair tumbled wildly past her shoulders, and she had a lovely hourglass silhouette, with curves that she saw as being overweight. She was a natural, unpolished beauty and she was completely oblivious of the fact - only making her more attractive, yet with her naivety making her even more vulnerable.

Anthony and Melissa sat on opposite couches. She placed a faux fur cushion on her stomach and wrapped her arms around it, then before long they were chatting without awkwardness. It genuinely felt like it had back when they were friends, back before she had lost herself along the way, and Melissa released the cushion from her tight grip.

"Are you ok? You look like you've been crying." Anthony looked concerned. She wasn't sure it was the best idea to trust in Anthony, but for some reason, she decided he was the one she was going to open up a little to; she actually couldn't help herself as she had bottled up her emotions for so long and in no time at all, she found herself pouring out her feelings as quickly as she had poured the wine earlier. As she talked and talked, he listened, and she felt a little lighter. She didn't go into everything of course, but she scratched the surface of the issue enough that it alleviated some of the weight she secretly carried around with her daily. She had soon talked her way through the crap and then they were laughing and joking, the mood much lighter. Then Anthony's phone went; it was Louisa and she needed picking up from town. Melissa felt a pang of sadness at the thought of him leaving, as she didn't particularly want to be alone again.

They said goodbye and she watched the headlights fade as he reversed off the driveway and headed down the cul de sac. As she gave a deep sigh, she felt another pang within her stomach. She glanced around the street; everywhere was so dark and still. It was past midnight now and the air was crisp. She looked up at the sky to a blanket of stars, uninterrupted by clouds. She had always been fascinated by the stars and found a certain magic in the night sky. Then it was there again, in the pit of her stomach, a strange twinge. Her body shuddered as she shut out the cold air, closing the door and returning to the warmth.

She picked up her phone; it was half-past twelve and she still hadn't heard from Chris. Tonight though, instead of feeling anxious, she wasn't fazed, especially now, her head was in a different place - a better place. She pulled out the ashtray from underneath the couch and lit a cigarette that lay in it, "I don't ask for much – do I? I'm not exactly high maintenance! I'm a good person, I know I am!"

"Why does he always treat me with such disregard? DISRESPECT?"

"Why do I keep putting up with it? What is wrong with me, for God's sake?" Her voice was getting louder and her frustration and confusion with herself was clear. With each question, she felt her emotions becoming more frenzied and each inhalation of smoke got more intense and deeper than the last.

"I can do better than him – Can't I? I'm not *that* bad-looking or *that* bad of a person, surely?" She broke away from the irate conversation that she was having with herself, as her phone beeped with a message. She reached out to grab her phone and opened the message, expecting it to be from Chris.

FROM ANTHONY - I had a really nice time tonight. Hope you're ok now, Night X

The strange pang in her stomach returned and it diffused her fury somewhat. 'Oh no,' she thought, 'I've had WAY too much wine! There is no way!' Half chuckling to herself, she dismissed the fact she had finally recognised the feeling in her stomach as the first flurry of butterflies you get when you like someone. She put the feeling solely down to the fact that she had consumed far too much wine. It wasn't unheard of for her to convince herself that she had fallen for any man that simply smiled at her the right way, let alone one that gave her a compliment. Dreaming of a different life, with a different love. It was a regular by-product of getting completely wasted on the occasional girly nights out, where she was granted a pass out from the clutches of Chris. It was an all too familiar pattern for Melissa, and with that, she decided that it was time to head off to bed and try and get to sleep before Chris returned.

Snuggled in her bed, she texted Anthony back.

TO ANTHONY – Yes, I am, Thank you. Night X

She deleted all the texts between them by force of habit; not because she felt she had done anything wrong, but because it wasn't worth the police-like interrogation that she suffered if any males (even if they were his or her family members) made contact with her, not to mention the torturous days of silent treatment that would follow. She turned off her bedside lamp and snuggled down, embedding her head comfortably into the pillow, and pulling the duvet right up over her shoulder. She smiled to herself - for the first time in a long time - as she closed her eyes, and before long, she was sound asleep.

CHAPTER 2.

COMING BACK TO LIFE

When the sound of her alarm pierced at her semi-hung-over head, she groaned as she blindly bashed her hand up and down over her bedside table. She tried desperately to locate her alarm clock to stop its grating sound - in doing so, all she did was knock it to the floor! She let out a loud yawn and attempted to open her sleep-fused eyes, rubbing at them as she sat up. She precariously leaned off the bed, grabbed the clock from the floor and switched off the alarm. "There!" She breathed a sigh of relief, as she sat back up. She glanced over at the other side of the bed; Chris's pillow still had the imprint of his head sunken into it and the duvet was all twisted - evidence that he had been home. As she leant over to brush out the creases in his pillow and straighten the duvet, she felt the warmth in the sheets. A wave a dread swept over her entire body. 'Could he still be downstairs?', she gulped, and her stomach began to tie itself in knots.

Chris lived the same cycle day in, day out; he would stay out until one or two o'clock in the morning, (doing God only knows what), he worked Monday to Friday, starting at seven most days and he played lower league rugby on a Sunday and Tuesday. He trained almost every night, fuelled by an extremely pushy and bolshy father, that, and his own delusions of grandeur that he would one day play in the super league, despite the fact he was fast approaching 26. His 'incredible' talent for the game was only really seen by his family, who all bragged about him as if he were the next Jonny Wilkinson. Melissa used to admire his tenacity and the unwavering belief that he held in his pursuit of his goals and dreams. She had always supported his need to train so much and attended all his games, but she had grown tired of it in recent years, as it ruled everything in his (and her) life. As reality began creeping in that he may not make it on a full-time professional level, it caused even more problems in their relationship. His bitterness and anger grew at his lack of success, and he took those frustrations out on Melissa. He always blamed her when he had a bad game; either she hadn't cooked him the right food that week, or it was because they had slept together the night before – despite him always initiating it. There was always something, always an excuse, but never the fact that he might just not have the ability to make it.

She candidly placed her foot on each step as she tiptoed downstairs, her stomach in knots. She had seen his car through the bedroom window, so she knew he was still at home. She would have much rather stayed in bed, but she would have been late for work and that was the one part of her life that she loved, so no matter what, she was not going to do anything to jeopardise that.

"What the FUCK is this!!" he bellowed, as she entered the lounge. Chris was stood in the middle of the room, ready for work, wearing a tight t-shirt to display his muscular arms and with his fair hair slicked back, overloaded with gel. He looked completely furious, and he was holding up the ashtray from last night – [the one thing she had stupidly forgotten to hide away in her tipsy state.] "WELL? I'm waiting!"

Like a small child in front of a headteacher at school, all her courage from last night disappeared. "I'm sorry, I should have moved it." She reached out her shaking hand to take it off him, but he hit her arm away, sending cigarette dimps and ash flying all over her and the floor. "Never mind you should have moved it! What are you doing smoking in MY HOUSE!" [It was, of course, their house, her name was on the mortgage too, something she had regretted almost immediately after they got the keys and almost every minute since they moved in 12 months ago. It was after this his controlling and abusive behaviour worsened.] "I...I...I just needed them, Chris; you'd left me alone again and said all of them horrible things..." she looked straight into his eyes, with tears gathering in her own, hoping for just an ounce of understanding. "Awwww, what a shame!" He tilted his head in a mocking manner, pulling his face like a baby; "You're PATHETIC and DISGUSTING and I leave you on your own because that's what you deserve!" He looked at her up and down in disgrace. "I can't even look at you; I wouldn't even mind as much if you lost weight from it, but you don't." He tipped the remains of the ashtray over her head and flung it to the side. "Now

CLEAN IT UP!!" he screamed, and with that he left the house, slamming the door behind him. It wasn't even half-past seven in the morning and Melissa was emotionally battered and bruised already.

She quickly tidied around, showered, tamed her mass of curls, put on some makeup, then took a deep breath as she picked up her car keys and left for work.

She arrived at work following another silent drive -she would never listen to the radio. That way, there was no chance that any tunes or lyrics could arouse emotions in her, that would consequently open the floodgates on the tears that she was trying so hard to harbour inside.

In company and on the surface, she smiled pretty much all day, every day, whilst on the inside, she spent most of her time fighting off demons and memories, just holding back tears. That was until recently, as she had now actually begun to genuinely enjoy the daytime when she was in work. Since starting her new job 6 months ago, she found that she could manage to completely block out her home life for at least seven blissful hours of the day.

She locked her car door and commenced the daily routine; using her outfit as a costume, her makeup as a mask, she felt empowered with each step, looking forward to seeing her colleagues that she had become so close with over the last 6 months. With each stride, she shed the upset of her home life, leaving it trailing behind.

The office was half-full when she arrived. "Morning, Honey!" shouted Colette chirpily. She was Melissa's senior at work, but they had quickly struck up an amazing friendship and they balanced the two wonderfully.

"Hey Col", Melissa replied. She really admired Colette (who was ten years older than her), as she seemed so together and focused. Colette was always the first one in the office, following an early morning session in the gym, and she was beyond efficient.

"Hi Mel, do you wanna grab a coffee?" shouted another voice, and out from the storeroom strutted a tall, slim, and extremely attractive woman, with long, poker-straight, raven-coloured hair - it was Liz. Liz was also always one of the first in the office, but unlike Colette, it was not so that she could gain a head start on her work, it was so she could grab whoever was willing to accompany her for a coffee and listen to her latest love life dilemma, sexual tryst or to delve into the drama of another.

Melissa looked over at Colette. "Do you mind, Col? I could really do with a coffee, actually?" Colette peered up from her computer screen, "Go for it lovely, you're not meant to start for another 30 minutes anyway!" she smiled, flicking her slightly wavy, mid-length, flaming amber hair over her shoulder, and quickly returning to beavering away in front of her computer.

The girls from the office would regularly gather at different points throughout the day. In the main, it would be at the coffee shop, which was two doors down from their building. Melissa was still feeling a little worse for wear and was in definite need of a caffeine fix, not to mention a good old moan to Liz - who would simply relish in giving her advice.

The air was crisp as they stepped outside; it was a fresh, spring morning. The sky was clear but the heat from the sun wasn't strong enough yet to provide any warmth, so Melissa shivered slightly as she fastened the buttons on her mac.

"Oooh – he's cute!" Liz pointed indiscreetly at a guy passing by, following him with a full head turn. Melissa giggled; Liz was completely man-mad, and she was extremely confident and immensely proud of her sexual prowess. Yet underneath her carefree exterior, she had a vulnerable side that she rarely showed. It left her open to obsessing about things in a slightly neurotic and exhaustive way, especially those closest to her.

As they entered the coffee shop it was a little warmer, homely. The hustle and bustle of town always made Melissa feel more alive, as she found something comforting in it. They grabbed two Mocha Choca Lattes with extra cream, which of course they would continually regret and moan about having throughout the day, as they did most days, yet they continued the daily ritual nonetheless. They removed their jackets, hanging them over the back of their chairs and sat down.

"So, what did that arse do last night then?" Liz asked inquisitively, as she blew into her cup of coffee before taking a sip – [the arse, of course, was Chris.]

"What do you mean?" Melissa replied, unconvincingly.

"Oh, come on hun, it doesn't take a rocket scientist to work out that you spent most of last night in tears, no matter how much concealer you put on babe!" Liz, who was also older than Melissa (by 12 years) was no stranger to the roller-coaster of crappy relationships and although on the surface seemed strong and in control, she had been played like a puppet for the past 8 years. She fell in love with a man who turned out to be married, Stephen, and he most definitely had her dangling on a string, continually lapping up one false promise after another. She dated other men throughout the 8 years, all the while convincing herself that she was the one in control and she wasn't putting her life on hold for a married man. However, nothing ever came from her other relationships as she could never seem to cut the feelings for Stephen out of her.

"Oh you know, just the usual", Melissa said as she began to divulge the night's events to Liz. For years, she had kept everything that happened behind closed doors all locked up inside her and completely hidden from sight, but there was something in Colette and Liz that made her feel like she could talk to them. Each day baring more and more. Liz was giving Melissa her full attention when Mel's phone beeped. "This is probably him now," she said as she reached into her coat pocket rolling her eyes. She rarely referred to Chris as anything other than 'him' these days – she hated the sound of his name. As she opened the message on her phone her tired eyes began to sparkle.

"Er, excuse me Missy, there is no WAY that *he* has made you smile like that, who is it? – SPILL!"

"Oh no, it's just a friend," replied Melissa dismissively, slightly unnerved by the fact that a simple text had made her smile so much. "It's Anthony, you know Louisa's boyfriend? He just called round last night and cheered me up. He's just texting to check I'm ok."

"Hmmm, he cheered you up did he?" Liz winked cheekily with a slight chuckle. "Well, what does it say?"

Melissa passed her phone over to a curious Liz, and she read the text aloud. "Morning, I hope you're ok today and showing off your lovely smile, it's too nice to hide away. No more tears. Xx" She paused momentarily, her eyes popping as she looked up from the phone and back at Melissa. "OMG – He likes you; he bloody likes you!!"

"No he doesn't! No way, No!" Instantly dismissing the speculations and she began to blush.

"Sweetie, it's *sooo* obvious, oh my god! How exciting!" Liz couldn't contain her excitement and was now physically bobbing up and down in her seat and grinning from ear to ear. "Is he cute?"

Melissa laughed as she found it highly amusing how little it took to excite Liz and she was also amused by the fact she thought Anthony could like her. "Liz, it's Chris's sister's boyfriend!" she held out her hand and raised her eyebrows gesturing 'point made'. Liz however, didn't alter her reaction. "And anyway, he most definitely does not like me!"

"But do you like him?"

"No! Stop it you, you're terrible!"

The question had never even crossed her mind, at least not before last night, but the return of those flutters in her stomach (that she had previously

29

passed off as too much wine) made her wonder? This sudden rush of blood that she was feeling was certainly more than a kick of caffeine.

Liz burst into song teasingly, "He loves you; he wants to kiss you, he wants to marry you!" They both fell about laughing.

"Shit! Look at the time!" Melissa gasped.

As always the gossiping had overrun and left them late for work. They jumped from their seats, linked each other's arms and rapidly-marched through the town's morning crowds back to work. All the way back Liz was deciding on the best way that Melissa could reply to the text, with Melissa just giggling at how crazy she was; it was just a text, after all?

Liz burst back into the office saying, "yes definitely, put that, play it cool, that's the best way." Melissa followed, glancing sheepishly at the clock, they were 10 minutes late. Colette peeped from behind her computer screen, noticeably looking at the clock, before fixating back at her computer screen.

"I'm really sorry Col", Melissa apologised, as she took off her jacket and handbag. She pulled back her office chair, at her desk opposite Colette, "we got distracted". Melissa hated being late; she was very conscientious and certainly didn't want Colette thinking that she was taking advantage of the fact they are friends. It was just that sometimes her mind wandered with much-needed distractions from the anguish of her home life.

Trying not to sound fazed, Colette insisted it was fine, yet she was clearly a little miffed. Col loved cocktails after work, but not coffees in work - she was far too ambitious and focused for that and it always took something big to break her out of work mode and into girly gossip, during the hours of 8-5, Monday –Friday.

"Yes, we got distracted because Mel has an admirer!" confessed Liz, who was the Team Leader in Marketing, so she didn't have to worry if she was late. Colette's ears pricked up; she could turn a blind eye to the usual girly tittle-tattle that was wittered on and off throughout the day, but a brand-new development - a new relationship or a break-up always caught her attention.

31

"What's this Mel?" she asked, unable to hide her intrigue.

"It's nothing, *really*! Liz is getting completely carried away with herself!" Melissa could feel herself blushing again, as a few of the other ladies in the office had turned their heads to hear what was going on too.

Liz began to give a rendition of the last 12 hours, in her own dramatic fashion, to the entire office and by the end of it all the other girls were demanding she sent a reply instantly so that they could all feast on the next instalment. An office debate began to be thrashed out about the rights and wrongs of affairs. With half the team stating it was different as Chris wasn't good enough for her and treated her terribly anyway so she deserved a bit of fun.

Melissa felt a bit disarmed by all the attention; she didn't even properly know all the girls yet – not to mention the fact that all the fuss was completely unfounded, as Anthony was completely smitten with Louisa and always had been.

She ignored all the suggestions she was given by everyone as to what she should text back and she just put what she felt was appropriate,

TO ANTHONY - Thank you, that's very kind. I am feeling better now, so thank you x.'

She received an almost instant reply,

FROM ANTHONY – "Not being kind just truthful, you do have an amazing smile xx"

Melissa looked stunned and slightly puzzled; were the girls, right?

"Well?" chorused an impatient Liz, Colette, and the other colleagues of Melissa's as they were huddled across the desk, looking on as excitedly as young birds awaiting a feed from their mother.

Melissa looked a little confused, so she simply passed her phone across to them, as they reached out impatiently. They all let out a shriek of excitement as they looked at the phone and began running away with themselves again. Melissa just couldn't understand where this was coming from - that's if it was, as it was beginning to seem - then it quickly dawned on her that if the girls were right, this could only mean trouble and she had enough of that already.

"What are you going to put back?" Liz, who was far too excitable over this for Melissa's liking, yelled.

"Nothing! There's no need to reply to that." Any lightheartedness or giddiness about the situation had drained away from her, as it had been overridden with worry and fear.

"Awwww!" they all chorused. Aside from Colette, the rest were unable to hide their disappointment.

"Anyway, I've got a meeting in a minute, so I need to get prepared." Melissa proclaimed.

"Yes, she's right, we have," Col backed her up and to Melissa's relief, she returned to work-focused Colette.

She put her phone in her handbag, put on her blazer, picked up her files and set off for the meeting with Colette, who didn't utter another word about it. Mel cleared her mind of all the nonsense – well, at least she tried to.

After a long, drawn-out meeting in a warm and stuffy meeting room, her hangover had reached a new level and she returned to the office in desperate need of a stodgy lunch. Colette had to stay on at the meeting whilst the managers summarised the next steps, so Mel returned alone. As she came through the office doors and headed towards her desk, a couple of the girls who were chatting with Liz, Colette, and herself this morning were flapping their hands to get her attention.

"That thing has not stopped since you left," they whispered. ['That thing' being Melissa's phone.] Mel delved into her handbag trying to find her phone amongst the million other, mainly useless items that she carried around daily. As she continued to rummage, she couldn't work out if her heart had just sunk or skipped a beat at the thought that it might be Anthony texting.

The sound of Liz shrieking overwhelmingly earlier echoed in her mind and she was only glad that she wasn't around right now. She had 5 messages, all of which *were* from Anthony. As she opened each one to read them, her stomach was flipping from butterflies to knots, as she could not quite believe what she was reading. She had probably always been a little naive, but she was far from stupid, and it was now plainly obvious that somehow, like a bolt out of the blue, Anthony, without any discretion was letting her know that he liked her and was seemingly testing the water to see if she had any feelings for him too.

The five texts basically rounded up to the message of how if Chris and Louisa were not brother and sister, then they should be together as they were just the same (behaviour-wise and the way they treated others). How Melissa was gorgeous, and she shouldn't have to put up with the way Chris treated her, and that all their friends thought the same, but no one was brave enough to stand up to Chris, and so on and so on.

Without the need for advice or reassurance, with her hands trembling, she instinctively typed a message back,

TO ANTHONY – I think you are getting ideas in your head that shouldn't be there and that you should stop texting now x

Just like the last time, she received an immediate response.

FROM ANTHONY - I know xx

She wasn't sure whether it was the hangover or all of the drama, but her head began to spin a little and she suddenly lost her appetite.

CHAPTER 3.

BREAKING THE RULES

In the staff room at lunchtime, Liz was adamant that they should all have an impromptu night out together. "Look, Mel, you have only been out with us, what twice? I mean, come on! Just tell Chris that it's someone's birthday or something, you had forgotten about it and that we are all insisting that you come along!"

Melissa raised her eyebrows and nervously pursed her lips as she deliberated over the prospect of going out; as appealing as it was, she wasn't sure she had the energy to deal with the fallout with Chris.

"Do you mean 'out out' Liz? On a school night?" Colette seemed slightly concerned at the prospect of a big midweek night out, knowing that the office productivity would be halved the next day!

"I'm in!" "Me too!" and "me too!" chirped up other voices from within the office.

"Yes Col, out out! We will have a toast to 'Miss pretty' here," nodding in Melissa's direction, with a mischievous smile. "Get smashed and have a little dance! We're only young, you know Col, bloody hell!" Liz could be likened to a female version of Peter Pan - the thought of anyone suggesting something might not be a sensible thing to do, or age-appropriate, only gave her further determination to do it anyway. "Come on you two!" Melissa and Col were firmly getting the eye from Liz now, and after exchanging a knowing glance between each other of the sort that says 'we're not going to get out of this', they agreed.

As they were going out straight from work, Melissa wanted to text Chris as soon as possible and try and smooth it over with him. She didn't want the worry about what she would be going home to playing on her mind the entire night.

TO CHRIS - SO SORRY I TOTALLY FORGOT ITS A GIRL FROM WORK LUCY'S BIRTHDAY MEAL TONIGHT, STRAIGHT FROM WORK AND I CAN'T GET OUT OF IT, I HAVE TRIED. I'M LEAVING THE CAR AT WORK AS HAVING A FEW DRINKS BUT I WON'T BE LATE XX

She let out a big sigh as she nervously awaited his response, which finally came around half an hour later.

FROM CHRIS - FINE MAKE SURE U R HOME BY 10 PM

She analysed the text - no kiss and a curfew on her time to get home meant that he wasn't in the best of moods, but it could have been worse, so she quickly replied 'OK' and went about the rest of her working day.

"Right girls, get your lippy on, it's cocktail o'clock and happy hour at James's Bar, so let's get our skates on!" Liz announced, eagerly whipping up the girls in the office.

When they arrived at the bar, it was typical of a Wednesday night - not too busy but there were enough people there to take advantage of the 2 for

1 cocktail offer. The sound of cheesy 90's pop music was playing from the DJ and his decks on the edge of the wooden dance floor, and the colourful disco lights were blinding at times. The girls danced and chatted before the cocktails had gone to their heads. The fact they had all decided to skip getting food helped them to enjoy a particularly cheap night and they proceeded to dance the night away, with their feet sticking to the pub floor as they skirted across it with their drinks held up in the air like accessories to their dancing.

"Shit! It's half 9!" Melissa said in a total panic.

"And...what's up Cinderella? Will your taxi turn into a pumpkin by midnight?!" Liz cackled, clearly finding herself extremely amusing.

Melissa couldn't help but giggle too; "No, ha, ha, seriously I need to go, Chris will go ape if I'm not back home by 10!"

"Oh screw him beautiful, and stay out; he'll get over it!" Although Liz knew a little about how Chris treated Melissa at times, she didn't know the half of it, no-one did.

Chapter 3. Breaking the Rules

"Honestly, it's fine, I'll just get a taxi." Melissa started to move away from the dance floor. She knew she had no time for goodbyes with everyone as they would only try and persuade her to stay and make it all the harder for her to get home. She didn't want to leave of course, she just didn't dare go home late.

She went outside to phone the taxi as she couldn't hear inside anyway and she thought it was a good opportunity to smoke the cheeky cigarette that she had hidden in the bottom of her work bag, in case of emergencies - obviously this was an emergency. Not only was she almost certainly not going to make it home on time, she was pretty drunk and was in desperate need of a cigarette at that precise moment. There was a slight nip in the air, and she couldn't distinguish whether it was smoke or simply her breath hitting the cold air each time a mini cloud formed with each breath she exhaled.

The taxi arrived, she got in and she watched on anxiously at the dashboard, as it seemed like both meter and the clock were on speed as she was travelling home. Time always dragged and the clock never seemed to even move when she was at home, but now, as she was desperate to make it home on time, it was like the clocks were laughing at her and going round at super-speed. At 10.15 pm, the taxi pulled up to her drive, she flung a £20 note in the driver's direction, shouting thank you, so as not to seem rude. As she bundled out of the door of the car whilst it was still yet to park up properly. She slammed the door and ran up the path as quick as her heels would carry her. She locked the front door behind her as quietly as possible. Eerily the house was in darkness, yet she knew Chris was home, a) because his car was on the drive but b) because there was no way he would set her a curfew and not be home to ensure that she stuck to it. She removed her heels, placing them by the front door and gingerly took each step upstairs. She went into the bathroom to get undressed down to her underwear, had a quick wash, and brushed her teeth to remove some of the smoke smell from herself before going into the bedroom. She tiptoed into the bedroom, and she couldn't believe her luck that he was fast asleep. She glanced at the clock; it was now 10.27 pm. Thank goodness he was asleep, or she would have been arguing until at least midnight. She carefully lifted the covers and climbed in. She was just snuggling down when she suddenly felt a huge thumping pain hit her back and bottom and the force of it threw her onto the bedroom floor. She raised her head up and tried to pull herself up onto her elbows. She looked up, bemused, and dazed by what had just happened, when there he was, with a face filled with fury - Chris staring right down at her. "You think you can just roll in at this time, and get into bed with me when you've been God knows where?" Chris was almost growling at her whilst glaring at her with utter disgust. "Chris, I'm not that late, it was the tax..." before she could finish, he snarled back at her, "NO! I don't want to hear your shit excuses; you can sleep on the floor like the dog that you are!" "But Chris!" she tried to approach him and reach out on to the bed, and he flung her off again; "and don't even think about getting in the spare bed or the couch or I'll come and set them on fire!" She was fairly sure he wouldn't ever go that far, but the mood he was in meant she wasn't going to try and find out whether he would or not. She watched as he turned over and slammed his body down onto the bed. She was shaken; her emotions almost numb from the shock, she was unable to react, cry, shout, or anything, she slowly laid down on the threadbare carpet, pulled her bare knees up towards her chest and she cradled as much of herself as she could. The longer she lay there, the more pins and needles kicked in from the hardness of the floor and her body became covered in waves of goosebumps, as the chill of the night air got under her skin. The tears began to flow, as she thought about how happy she had been only a couple of hours earlier, and then her thoughts turned to Anthony. She couldn't imagine that he would ever treat Louisa like this, and that familiar pang returned as she hoped that what the girls thought would be true. She could hear Chris snoring and she decided to creep to get her dressing gown off the back of the door so she could use it as a cover. The floorboards creaked as she reached a standing position and placed her first step. Chris flung his body around in the bed, disturbed by the noise yet still sleeping. She was so scared of waking him, she was so cold now and desperately needed something to cover her through the night. She successfully managed to unhook the dressing gown from off the hook on the back of the door and she quietly tiptoed back to the side of the bed and lay down on the floor. She curled up in a ball and snuggled as much of her body under the dressing gown as she could. She did of course contemplate trying to have a least a few hours' sleep in the spare room or on the couch; she considered setting her alarm to wake her before Chris's was set, but the fear of him waking stopped her. Although Chris had never carried out any of his extreme threats, she had never tested him by not obeying his requests in the first place. So she never quite knew just exactly how far he would go. Her eyes were tired from crying and she felt exhausted by the emotional ups and downs of the whole day and night. Her eyes began to close, and somehow, she fell asleep.

CHAPTER 4.

BOLT FROM THE BLUE

Melissa pushed around the cornflakes in her bowl, whilst looking across the table at Chris, watching as he slopped and slurped his way through a mouthful of cereal and toast. She had barely slept a wink all night, her body ached from sleeping on the hard floor and her mind was exhausted by the thoughts that had kept her awake on and off throughout the night. She kept saying 'I know' to herself, over and over, trying to work out if it could be interpreted any other way than the obvious – alarmingly, she also couldn't get pictures of Anthony's face out of her head, and thoughts of how different her life could be if he did truly like her.

"Are you not hungry?" Chris asked, "It's not like you to miss a meal", he grinned smugly to himself, as he proceeded to dip his toast into a giant mug of tea! Melissa's stomach churned and she heaved a little; each day she found him more and more repulsive. At times, she felt she was becoming more immune to his nasty jibes and put-downs – that, or perhaps she was just numb altogether. Of course, there was nothing wrong with Melissa's weight; she was a healthy size 12 with curves in all the right places. She didn't see this; naturally, after years of swipes at her weight, she spent most of her time taking up fad diets and avoiding full-length mirrors. It wasn't uncommon for him to state that she was so fat that she looked pregnant. He would then insist that she did some sit-ups, and he would proceed in standing over her until she reached her 'target'! It was only when she mentioned this a few months ago to Colette and Liz at work, that alarm bells went off with them and they had been attempting to build Melissa's confidence ever since, hoping to help her to see the light.

"Right, I'm off!" he announced loudly, as he got up from the table. Letting out an almighty burp, he grabbed Melissa's face with both his large hands - as if he knew she wanted to turn away - and he kissed her. Her nausea returned. She watched him walk away from the table and leave the kitchen. He had acted as if last night or yesterday morning hadn't happened, like it was normal, although she second-guessed herself a lot and often tied herself up in knots by trying to figure out if it was his behaviour that was unreasonable or hers. She was beginning to see the light and realise the situation she was in was far from 'normal' or healthy.

Melissa knew she had to leave Chris; (deep down she had known it for at least 12 months now). She hated him touching her, kissing her, just the mere sight of him these days; she just didn't know how to escape. Every time she had threatened it, his behaviour would change, just long enough for her to see the Chris she fell for in the first place and just long enough to pull her right back to square one, where she believed (hoped) that he would change. One of his last promises had been that it would be better once they were living together.

She shuddered as she wiped away the toast crumbs that he'd left on her face and began to clean up the breakfast pots. Her thoughts turned to Anthony again, and she reached into her pocket for her phone. She knew it was wrong and that she could be opening a huge can of worms, but she couldn't stop herself…...and she texted him –

TO ANTHONY – I CAN'T STOP THINKING ABOUT WHAT YOU SAID, I'M CONFUSED TO BE HONEST

She paused, biting softly at her lips. 'What am I doing?', she questioned herself, but she was stuck, and something had to change; she needed something to pull her away from this situation she found herself cemented in. As dangerous as it may have been, maybe this was her chance. She continued typing her text.

…I DON'T KNOW WHAT ELSE TO SAY X

SENT.

As she placed the phone down on the side, she could literally hear her heart thumping and increasing in speed, and it felt like it was about to burst out of her chest. After a few minutes, he still hadn't replied, yet the reply had been instant yesterday and she began to feel foolish, had she misread the signals? Had she been listening to the girls too much?

Frantically slapping on her makeup, her usual self-questioning provoked her anxiety, onto the verge of hyperventilating, then she noticed the time. It was only half-past seven; 'Of course, he will be with Louisa!' she realised. As a wave of relief washed over her, it was shortly followed by the return of anxiety when the realisation he was very possibly with Louisa simply reaffirmed just how explosive this situation could end up and how out of hand it could all get. She really didn't understand her own behaviour and this sudden magnetic-like force that she now felt towards Anthony. It had been less than 48 hours and it felt like her whole world was being, or was on the verge of being, turned upside down.

As she'd left her car at work, she just got a taxi. The sound of the rain pouring down on the car was almost deafening and she could barely see out of the windows, despite the windscreen wipers going at full speed. She was glad she wasn't the one who had to concentrate on getting her to work in one piece, as she couldn't stop her mind from wondering why Anthony hadn't replied. The taxi pulled up as near to her work as possible, but just as she was about to step out, the rain seemed to fall even heavier. She quickly left the car, throwing up her brolley and 'tooted', as she called it, (attempting to run in heels) to her works building. As she entered the entrance to the building, she put down her umbrella and quickly wiped her feet. Certain that she had felt her phone vibrate, she took it out to have a look. There it was her long-awaited reply from Anthony. She read the words and she couldn't take them in. She stood dumbfounded in the middle of the entrance. People were rushing past her to escape the rain, and someone barged right into her, tutting loudly at her obstruction. She hazily came round from her shock-induced daze. She headed towards the lift, with her mind otherwise occupied and she didn't notice the wet floor sign in the lobby. As her stiletto shoes hit the slippy tiles, she looked like a scene from Bambi and consequently ended up on her derrière - which was now also wet and not in the most flattering of places.

Staff from other departments rushed to her aid and helped her into the lift, seeing her right to her office to make sure she was okay. Still feeling slightly out of sorts, not to mention completely mortified by her fall, at least she could now pass off her dazed state as shock from falling over.

The staff explained to Colette and Liz what had happened, and they immediately began to fuss over her asking if she was ok, had she hit her head? - not that she was taking anything in; everything they were saying seemed just like a distant noise.

"He said he's in love with me!" she blurted out suddenly, "and he has been for the past two years!"

"Who has, Anthony? Anthony? I take it we're talking about Anthony. Jesus, no wonder you fell over!" Liz grinned from ear to ear, as she got visibly giddier with each repetition of the word Anthony. "What did I tell you, Missy! Woo hoo!" Anyone would have thought that she had just been told "I love you" herself, from the way that she was dancing around.

53

"Really Mel? Well, bloody hell, eh!" Colette's reaction was a lot more muted. "I think this warrants a coffee. You just stay here; I'll grab us some to take away and we'll go into the meeting room where we can talk."

Still slightly in a whirl from the last ten minutes, Melissa nodded her head, "I just can't.... I can't believe it! He can't mean it - surely? I mean, it must be a game or something? I just don't understand!"

When Colette returned with their coffees, the three of them headed off to the meeting room, complete with their files - just to make it look official of course. Just as she did yesterday, Melissa handed over the phone to them so they could read the messages themselves, rather than suffer the rash of embarrassment rearing its ugly head and creeping like red vines up her neck.

Colette and Liz seemed to be just as shocked as she was as they read his text. They thought he was after a bit of a fling, but neither of them had expected a profession of love! The girls spent an hour chatting away; was he genuine or a love rat? Did Melissa like him? Should she pursue it? How should she respond? What about Louisa? What would happen if Chris found out? Typical 'girl talk', logical questions but completely strung out, meaning, the best way to avoid getting back to work. Melissa was mainly surprised that they didn't think Louisa and Chris should even factor in how she decided to move forward with the situation. They just dismissed them as deserving everything they got, from what they knew of them. What surprised Melissa even more, was that she didn't seem to care either, not really. There was no love lost between her and Louisa, not since that fateful girls' trip to Cyprus, along with several things that had happened since then, and Chris had destroyed all the feelings that she had for him all on his own. It was then it dawned on her, that she was seriously contemplating this and that somewhere, somehow, she *must* have felt something for Anthony. Maybe that is why she was so hurt by his 'supposed' betrayal all those years ago, and the reason that she had felt such anger towards him ever since. The last thing she was going to do, however, was to profess her love straight back. She wasn't even definitely sure she liked him for a start, never mind love him! There was also the fact that the cynical side of her (that had developed from all the years of Chris's mind games), meant that something was niggling at her; this could just be a trick, a sick game that they were all in on, designed to test her. She knew it seemed far-fetched – crazy almost, but she wouldn't put anything past Chris these days, (not after some of his antics), and she had always thought of Anthony as a bit of a lap dog to Louisa, so she was pretty sure he would do or say whatever they wanted him to. She just didn't know who to trust. 3 days ago, Anthony barely spoke to her and now he was declaring his love for her? She was so confused, and she wanted to keep her guard firmly up. She didn't want to think that way and when she hinted at that scenario to the girls, they looked at her like she had completely lost the plot.

"Sweetie, is that incomprehensible to you that someone might actually like you, love you? I mean, have you looked in a mirror recently? Not that it's all about looks, I mean you're one hell of a babe, inside and out you know?"

Melissa blushed and shook her head, dismissing the compliments.

"That's the thing with you, lovely, you genuinely don't see how blooming special you are. Liz is right and there's a load of guys in this building who would love the chance to take you out!"

Mel smiled; she wasn't convinced, by any means, but maybe believing what Anthony had said wasn't as far-fetched as believing it was a setup. She couldn't and wouldn't get thrust into this giant tornado, just because of the unexpected romance of it all though. After all, what did he want - one night of passionate love? An affair? She wasn't capable of that! To run off into the sunset together. Marriage? Her thoughts kept running away with her.

`I just need to really think about this,' she thought to herself. At the tender age of 22, she felt she had already made way too many mistakes and was so terrified of making anymore. One thing that she did know though, after the humiliation of last night, the boost of this couldn't have been more perfectly timed!

She sent a brief reply in text to Anthony-

TO ANTHONY - Well I wasn't expecting that! Don't really know what to say... xx

She replied because she felt she should say something, but she didn't interact with him any further or give any indication of her own feelings - other than the double kiss, after only ever putting one before now.

In the week following Anthony's declaration of love, Melissa's feelings began to grow, and her barrier slipped down gradually day by day. With each move he made; she couldn't help but fall deeper. She felt like she was in a real-life game of chess, and at any moment, he was about to shout 'check' and she'd be powerless to do anything but succumb to his advances.

Her evenings would be spent as an emotional punchbag, (dependant on Chris's mood swings) and her days would be filled with messages that would lift her mood and confidence, that would make her feel a little more alive each day. She found that she wasn't drinking as much, just a couple of glasses in the evening with her tea or for pleasure - rather than the couple of bottles a night that she had previously been consuming in order to numb her pain. Chris's insults seemed to bounce off her of late too, leaving her 'only' bruised, rather than chipping away at her soul and adding to her internal scarring. On the nights that she knew Anthony wouldn't be with Louisa, she would long for Chris to have one of his outbursts and storm out leaving her alone, just so that she could spend the night chatting to Anthony - she would have to 'one-bell' him of course, in order for him to know that the coast was clear to phone her. She could never have rung him and allowed it to connect since Chris checked her phone bill far too often and she was already worrying about explaining the increase in her texts to him (so much so that Liz was letting her use her phone in the day). However, given that this lust-driven relationship was growing by the day, using other people's phones and trying to limit texts was far from ideal. She would have loved to have been able to chat over text so much more in the daytime. She could have sworn that her heart quite literally skipped a beat every time she went to her phone and there was a text waiting for her from him. They were slipping into sending more and more though, despite the risks, (routinely deleting the texts at the end of each day); they could not seem to help themselves.

CHAPTER 5.

A TRUTH UNCOVERED

FROM ANTHONY - CAN I SEE YOU? I WANT TO SAY ALL THESE THINGS FACE TO FACE. I WANT...I NEED YOU TO BELIEVE ME xxx

It had been a whole week and her feelings were growing rapidly - that was now becoming increasingly obvious from her texts, but equally, she was slightly keeping her guard up - although her vulnerability was becoming clearer by the day. As each day passed, Anthony convinced her a little more that his feelings for her were completely genuine. Every text, that was bursting with compliments and nothing but positivity, was like a wrecking ball taking down her walls, despite her desperately trying to keep them up. She knew she couldn't just hide behind her phone forever, just exchanging flirty texts in order to make her feel happier. It was time to meet him and she knew it - how she could do it safely though, was another thing entirely?

TO ANTHONY - I DO THINK WE SHOULD MEET, WE DEFINITELY NEED TO TALK IN PERSON... BUT WHERE? WHEN? XX

Melissa glanced at the wall clock in the office - it was 11am. She tried to think of a time and place in which it would be safe for them to meet; just then, her phone beeped again.

FROM ANTHONY - HOW ABOUT DINNER? 12:30 PM? I'LL PICK YOU UP xxx

Mel's stomach flipped and a beaming smile consumed her face. She took a deep breath, 'Am I ready for this?' she questioned herself. Whether she was or she wasn't, she found herself already replying.

TO ANTHONY - IT SOUNDS PERFECT, BUT WHAT ABOUT WORK? WILL THEY LET YOU OFF-SITE THAT LONG? xx

FROM ANTHONY - YOU LET ME WORRY ABOUT THAT! SEE YOU THEN! :) XXXX

TO ANTHONY - OK SEE YOU LATER THEN. :) PHONE ME WHEN U R HERE xx

Smiling to herself, Melissa put her phone back into her handbag and turned back towards her computer and tried her hardest to focus on work, so that it wasn't the longest hour and a half in history.

"ARGHHH!! I can't stand that jumped up little...", Colette screamed with frustration as she stormed through the office door and slammed her folders onto her desk.

"What's up, Col?" Melissa didn't often see Colette so worked up, there was only really little cocky Ed in Sales that wound her up at work. Him and the ever-present third wheel - AKA Katrina - in her relationship with her husband Martin, that would wind her up at home. Like Melissa, Colette was also a Libra and whether there was anything in star signs or not, they both were quite balanced people, easy-going people by nature, although, at times, the littlest thing could tip the scales.

"Oh, nothing lovely, you know what that bloody Ed is like, knocking back all of our Marketing campaign proposals before he's even listened properly! It's just so he can exercise his authority over me, and it drives me flipping mad! But I'm over it now lovely, ...deep breaths ...ahhhh...that's better, are you ok?"

"Yes, I'm good, well nervous, but good, well not entirely nervous; I'm excited too, but...."

"Nervous? Why lovely?" Colette interrupted, looking intrigued.

"It's Anthony; he's coming to pick me up at 12.30. We're finally meeting, well obviously we've met before, I mean I've known him for years, but you know what I mean", she nervously rambled, "I mean, since he told me that he, you know...loved me."

"Oooohh! Bloody hell, lovely! It's ten to 12 now! You better get ready!"

"Ready into what? I've only got these clothes!"

"Oh honey, you look lovely, but I just mean you'll want to freshen up. You might want to get close, you know, and you'll want to feel nice when you do!"

"Oh?" Melissa looked even more nervous than she was before.

"Oh honey, don't worry, I just mean, brush your teeth, wipe under your arms and you know," Col continued by gesturing her eyes towards Melissa crotch area.

"Col, flipping 'eck! I'm not going to need to freshen up down there!" Melissa shrieked quite defensively. "What do think I am? We're just going to chat, but in person this time." It may have been naive of her, but her statement of her intentions was completely true. She had absolutely no intention of conducting any sort of passionate tryst the first time of them meeting face to face - especially in his car during her lunch hour. The thought of it felt completely sordid and she never wanted to feel like that again. As her past haunted her thoughts, she shook them away as quickly as they had entered her head. She knew that this was nothing like that; even if something did happen this lunchtime, however, that was not what she wanted from this meeting at all.

"I don't think you're like anything Mel, but this guy really likes you and you like him, so you know, sometimes these things happen. Please don't be offended honey."

"I'm not, don't worry, sorry, I just won't be doing that, don't worry." She was a little offended, but that was through her own demons, not through what Colette had said.

Before she knew it, Anthony had rang to say he was there. She nervously made her way to the car to meet him. When she saw his face, it was like she was seeing him for the first time, she was so attracted to him, she noticed things about him that she never had before - she was seeing him in a whole new light.

They sat and chatted. The more that he told her about how Louisa treated him with such little respect, only convinced her further that both Chris and Louisa had brought this on themselves.

Anthony also told Melissa that Chris had been seeing another girl - which only confirmed what she had already thought for so long, to the point that it had driven her demented - and Chris seemingly enjoyed tormenting her with it.

She had found one of his phone bills whilst tidying up one day, around 6 months ago and it was only the fact that near enough one page of it was filled with another number (that wasn't hers) and times that the messages were sent, that she decided to look into it further. When she searched for the number and found that it wasn't in her phone, she even rang the number and a girl answered.

Her blood began to boil, and her breath quickened. Anthony had just reaffirmed all her suspicions. He told her how long it had been going on for and just how many of 'their group' knew about it. She wasn't angry because she cared, the feelings raged as she recalled how Chris had treated her all this time. All the times she begged him for the truth, and all he would do is laugh at her, mocking her and saying she would never know. She felt dizzy as she thought about all the times that she'd been made to sleep on the floor, beg for forgiveness, miss out on nights out. Punished for years for things she hadn't done. Relentlessly accused of cheating, when all the while it was him that was cheating! A whirring of anger, embarrassment, and sadness swirled around inside of her. As Anthony continued to talk, reiterating that she was so just too good for Chris anyway. It was like a strike of lighting; she *was* too good for Chris and knowing the truth about him had helped to finally flick the switch of any feelings that she may have still had for him firmly into the off position.

"Are you OK? I'm sorry, I just thought you should know. That's why I wanted to see you in person. I know you are fighting what you feel for me because you feel bad on Chris, but you shouldn't, he doesn't deserve you, Lissy" She had never heard him call her that before, and it felt more serious than calling her Zippy. No-one called her that, other than her family, and she liked it.?

Melissa looked right into Anthony's eyes; they were a piercing blue; she felt a physical reaction to gazing into his eyes like they had hypnotic qualities. It was right there and then she realised that her guard had dropped completely. He *was* being genuine and she could feel it. She was 22 years old, and her life had felt so heavy, sad and serious for as long as she could remember. She just wanted to be happy, to have fun and be carefree, if only for a while. Still staring into Anthony's eyes, she felt a pull towards him. With a knowing smile, he leant towards her too and their lips met for the first time. The kiss built up gradually, starting gently and growing with passion as he placed his hands on either side of her face. Even though it probably should have felt wrong, it felt so right. She got completely lost in the embrace and it was Anthony who pulled away first. With his hands still gently placed on either side of her face, he looked straight into her eyes again.

"You don't have to say anything, I know you're not there yet, but I love you Lissy."

She smiled and nervously looked down; she was never very good at accepting compliments and this was one hell of a compliment.

"Look at me, I mean it!" he stately boldly, whilst lifting her chin so that her eyes met his again. He was smiling and her smile grew even bigger as he leaned in to kiss her again.

Until that point, she had put off seeing Anthony face to face - she didn't trust herself not to fall straight into his arms. Of course, she had been right not to trust herself, she had just fallen straight into his arms, but she was now convinced that his feelings towards her were true - and even if they weren't, right now, she didn't really care. She had eradicated any thoughts that this was a trap set by Chris. All she could think about was Anthony and how he managed to make her feel happier and more confident than she had felt in a long, long time.

CHAPTER 6.

DIFFERENT FROM ALL THE REST

Melissa had spent the afternoon following her lunch meet up with Anthony on cloud nine.

She felt so happy, however intermittent pangs of anger, fuelled by the concrete knowledge of Chris's infidelity, kept creeping in. She just couldn't believe that throughout all these years, he had treated her like dirt for supposedly cheating so many times, when all the while he had been judging her by his own behaviour. Anthony had given her a SIM card that she could put in her phone whilst she was at work, so that they could talk as much as they wanted to throughout the day. Strangely, she didn't feel sneaky or wrong accepting it - especially not after hearing about Chris's cheating ways. In fact, she had texted Chris immediately to say that they'd had a big meeting at work and that they now had to switch their phones off during the day. She didn't even wait for his reply before switching her SIM card over and then spending the rest of the day exchanging endless messages with Anthony. Between lusting after Anthony and driving herself insane with anger at wasted years with Chris, it probably would have been better for her career if work had instilled the 'no phone' rule, as she was not getting much work done at all!

She felt like she couldn't even face going home that night, as she knew she wouldn't be able to contain her feelings. If Chris had any inkling though, that she knew about him and his 'floozy', he would have interrogated her SAS-style. If he even so much as thought that it was Anthony who was the whistleblower, then World War Three would erupt and it wouldn't be Chris who would come off worse. He would only try wriggling his way out of it anyway and deny any wrongdoing, so there was no point saying anything and she didn't want to do anything that might put Anthony at risk. She decided the safest thing to do was to call to her Dad's after work and she would wait there until she knew that Chris would have left for training before returning home. That way she wouldn't have to see his lying, cheating face.

She hugged and kissed the girls in the office goodbye - Colette and Liz had a managers' meeting so they were staying on late tonight. She made her way to the car park with a few of her colleagues, saying goodbye when she reached her car. She began thinking about the last two weeks and the radical changes she had seen and felt within herself. She felt she was shedding herself of her insecurities, becoming braver and less confused about who she was, each and every day. She still had a long way to go and a lot of healing to do, but her passion for Anthony was putting a new-found spring in her step and her sense of betrayal by Chris put a purpose in her stride.

She collapsed into her car slamming the door behind her, then swiftly locking it. She reached over and placed her designer handbag in the passenger footwell. (The handbag was just one of many 'guilt gifts' that Chris would shower her with, in an attempt to show he had changed whenever she'd

73

threatened to end their relationship). She caught a glimpse of herself in the rear-view mirror as she leant back towards the driver's side. She stared for a moment and smiled, a smile she hadn't seen before; it was poised with menace. Her initial instinct was to plot revenge, as she could feel her soul filling up with a burning hatred. The fire was quickly distinguished with a wave of sadness that washed over her. She still couldn't understand how Chris could have treated her so badly, how he could be so cruel towards her; she had never done anything to deserve it. Looking away from the mirror before she cried, she was just about to start her car when her phone beeped. She reached over into her bag to get her phone.

FROM ANTHONY - CALL AT YOUR DADS TONIGHT ON YOUR WAY HOME FROM WORK XX

TO ANTHONY - THAT'S SO WEIRD! IT'S LIKE YOU READ MY MIND! THAT'S EXACTLY WHAT I AM DOING XX

After replying, she then wondered why it was that he was suggesting she went there anyway.

TO ANTHONY - WHY DO SAY THAT ANYWAY? X

FROM ANTHONY - WAIT AND SEE ;) XXX

She felt a whole flurry of flutters jumping around her stomach, and she was awash with excitement. She was intrigued as to what it was, he had up his sleeve. She was in completely unknown territory, but she liked it.

She turned on her ignition and put the radio on, unafraid of what song she may hear, what lyrics they would include or what feelings they would trigger. She loved music and she needed to embrace it again. As she pulled out of the car park, and her lane of traffic came to a standstill, Beyoncé's 'Crazy in Love' blasted from the speakers. She smiled at the irony of this song coming on at that moment, on that day. She suddenly found herself lost in the song, shaking her bum in her seat and rolling her shoulders, dancing away. Completely unfazed by the looks of the passengers in the cars in the next lane - just the way she used to be! She laughed to herself as she sang along to the odd words that she knew and humming away to the rest of it.

Chapter 6. Different from All the Rest

As she pulled into the driveway of her childhood home, she felt an immediate sense of peace and belonging, just as she always had when she returned here. Colette and Liz had once questioned why she wouldn't just return home and leave Chris, reassuring her there was no shame in admitting it hadn't worked out. That wasn't the reason Melissa didn't return home though. She knew she didn't have to worry about what her family would think about it not working. Her dad never even wanted her to get a mortgage so young - nor was he Chris's number-one fan. Her dad, Pete, had never thought that Chris was good enough for Melissa anyway, not that he even knew the half of what went on, he just never felt that he treated her as well as he should have done. Melissa thought the world of her dad and never wanted to burden him with any of the hurt or pain that she had gone through. Mel's parents had split when she was in her mid-teens, and she and her younger sisters stayed with their dad in the family home. Not long after, their Mum was offered a job in Scotland which meant that it was months in between them seeing her. Also, their dad was crushed by this fact, as it meant they would never reconcile their marriage.

It had taken Melissa's dad four years before he was ready to find love again. Mel and her sisters were ecstatic when he did find someone again, not to mention the fact that his new love, Linda, could not have been more perfectly suited to her dad Pete. However, unfortunately, it was not the happy ending they all longed for. Not long after the whirlwind engagement and wedding of her dad and Linda, the cracks began to show. Linda's behaviour became more and more irrational. Linda turned out to be an alcoholic and she would swing from the nicest, most welcoming of women, to Cinderella's wicked step mum within moments. Melissa and her sisters felt sad and helpless as they watched their beloved dad try and save a doomed marriage. As Linda had always refused to seek the help she so desperately needed. The happy childhood home they had all grown up in, now made for a very turbulent and destructive one for Pete, Jenny, and Gemma (Melissa's sisters). Mel had once hinted at the fact she may want to return home, but it was met with a very noticeable panic and nervousness from her dad and she quickly retracted her request. 'U-turning' and completely playing down how unhappy she was. Her dad had suffered, and was still suffering enough stress in his life and she certainly didn't want to add to his troubles in any way at all.

Thankfully, Linda, who worked in retail, was on a late tonight so she wouldn't be home until 8.30 pm, so for at least a couple of hours, 'home' was relaxed and reminiscent of their childhood days. She was sitting enjoying watching TV with her sisters whilst her dad was cooking tea, when there was a knock at the door.

Pete left the pan on the stove and went to answer it. Thinking nothing of it and laughing away at the TV, Pete shouted, "Lissy, they're for you!"

"What are?" She shouted back towards the hall. She had forgotten herself, lost in the comfort and warmth of her sister's and dad's company, then it dawned on her what Anthony had texted her. She suddenly panicked; she didn't want her dad to think badly of her; what had Anthony done?

Her dad entered the room with a big bouquet of ruby red roses. She sprang from the settee, partly with excitement, partly with embarrassment.

"Who they from? Never known Chris do anything like this and it's not like it's Valentine's Day?" questioned Pete, suspiciously.

"I don't know, and he does do nice things sometimes, Dad," she replied, unconvincingly.

She frantically opened the card, hoping they weren't from Chris. If he started one of his random nice patches, it would just totally confuse her.

'I can't stop thinking about you, A xxx'

She was unable to hide the smile that instantly embraced her face - she would now have to explain who 'A' was, as Jenny and Gemma had teasingly snatched the card from her hands.

"A, who's A, hmmm? Not Adam Frodsham from school?" Gemma asked, unimpressed.

"No!!" Melissa snapped back with a grimace.

"Hmmm, who then, A, A…. Anthony! Yes, I've always said he liked you!" Melissa could feel the blood rushing to her cheeks, and she smiled nervously; she couldn't help it. "It is! You're smiling, that's it, it's Anthony!" Gemma stated, with her eyes and mouth wide open, extremely excited by the whole thing. Jenny was less giddy and smiling more so at Melissa's embarrassment; she was the most laid back and demure of the three sisters. Melissa was known for her crazy ways (although not of late) and Gemma was a fiery little pocket rocket.

"No, don't be daft," once again Melissa replied, rather unconvincingly. "I don't know who they are from!"

Pete looked at her questionably, with a knowing look. "OK, it is Anthony, I don't know what's got into him, he thinks he likes me, but he doesn't. I'll tell him not to do anything like this again, it will all be fine!" Melissa nervously mumbled as she left the living room, clutching her phone and typing away. She could hear her sisters as she left the room, "I knew it," proclaimed Gemma. "Calm down," instructed Jenny. Pete followed Mel out of the back room and returned to cooking the tea.

Melissa went into the front room, her fingers shaking as she typed, her smile was ear to ear. She was embarrassed that she had been forced into admitting something to her dad, but she was bowled over by the gesture - she wasn't used to being on the receiving end of anything even slightly romantic, so it didn't take much to sweep her off her feet.

TO ANTHONY- I GOT THE ROSES, THANK YOU :) XXX

She stared at her phone, just waiting for his reply.

FROM ANTHONY - DID YOU NOTICE THE WHITE ROSE, THAT'S BECAUSE YOU ARE DIFFERENT FROM ALL THE REST. XXX

She chuckled to herself; she thought they must have just been one short of the red roses, so had stuck a white one in. Anthony's romantic nature tugged at her heartstrings, and it was something she could definitely get used to.

She sat around the table with her dad, Jenny, and Gemma; they had Rod Stewart records playing in the background (Pete's favourite), and they were all singing and laughing as they tucked into a big bowl of pasta bolognese and overloaded themselves with garlic bread, whilst Pete overdid it on the Peter Kay garlic bread jokes. It felt like heaven, and she wished that she could have stayed there forever, that her relationship with Chris, the mortgage, everything, would just disappear. She wished that she could wave a magic wand and make Linda better so that she would be the wife her dad deserved. Then, it suddenly dawned on her that it was a quarter to eight.

"Shit! It's quarter to 8!" she exclaimed.

"Oh bugger, I better bloody tidy up and go!" On edge as to what mood Linda would be in when she returned home from work was the main reason she had to 'escape'. She knew, as they all did, Linda always hit bottle as soon as she got home - so as much as Pete loved Melissa, he didn't try and stop her as he desperately wanted to do anything he could to prevent another drunken outburst .

"I'm off to my room then," sighed Gemma, as she kissed Melissa goodbye.

Melissa hugged Jenny and her dad, desperate to get in the car as she'd remembered she still had her new SIM card in her phone and needed to switch it over before she aroused any suspicion.

As she went darting out the door, Pete shouted after her, "what about these roses, are you not taking them?"

"Of course not, bloody hell, Dad! Jenny, you and Gem have them, I can't take them," and with that, she dashed out of the door.

She sat in the car on the drive whilst she switched over the SIM cards, breathing a sigh of relief. Whilst she tried to think of a safe place to hide it, her phone starting pinging non-stop.

FROM CHRIS - WHERE ARE YOU? X

FROM CHRIS - HELLO WHERE ARE YOU?

FROM CHRIS - WHERE THE FUCK ARE YOU AND WHERE IS MY TEA??

FROM CHRIS - YOU SLAG!!!! I DON'T KNOW WHO YOU THINK YOU ARE NOT COMING HOME OR NOT ANSWERING ME!! HOW DARE YOU!!

She let out a big sigh - "Charming as ever, Chris!" she said aloud to herself, when she was suddenly startled by frantic beeping from a nearby car. Jumping out of her skin, she whizzed around thinking it would be Chris trying to track her down. Instead, it was Linda, with a face like thunder and frantically gesturing for Melissa to move off the drive. Melissa raised her hand to indicate one minute and mouthed sorry to her - to which Linda shook her head and rolled her eyes! As she was reversing off the drive her phone started ringing again and again until she answered it.

"Hello!"

"Hello, are you fucking kidding me? Hello? Just what do you think you're playing at and just who are you playing with? You slapper!"

"For God's sake, Chris, I've been at my dads for tea, I forgot to switch my phone back on after work, end of story." She felt slightly uneasy telling lies, although the fact it wasn't all lies and the way he was speaking to her did make it easier.

"Oh really?" he replied, seemingly calming down, yet still harbouring an arrogant tone.

"Yes really! For God's sake, Chris, it's more like who do you think you are? Talking to me like that?

Calling me a slag, for what, eating tea with my dad and sisters?"

"You what?" Taken aback by her turning the argument around on him, he cut the conversation dead. "Oh, fuck off. I'm going training!" The line went dead.

"Eeeeeeerrrrrrrrrrrrrrrrr!!!!!!" She let out a disgruntled scream and banged the steering wheel.

BEEP BEEP! She still hadn't moved far enough away from the drive after Chris distracted her.

"OK OK, keep your knickers on!" She drove off giving Linda the finger - out of plain sight of course, but it made her feel better. Between Chris and Linda, she felt terribly wound up with nowhere to direct her anger, despite her day also including the most perfect first kiss with Anthony and those special roses, and a lovely family tea. Her peace had been so quickly taken away and her first stop on the way home was the off licence for a bottle of red and a packet of cigarettes. She still had to think of somewhere to put this 'dangerous' SIM card; she felt like had a stick of dynamite in her hands.

Chapter 6. Different from All the Rest

CHAPTER 7.

A LINE CROSSED

It was a Friday night and she was staying at Liz's. Colette was coming also, as they were all going to an R 'n B night at a club near Liz's house in Didsbury, and they started on the vino early whilst they got ready. Amongst a raft of other gossip, of course, the subject of Melissa and Anthony was firmly on the agenda.

"Have you not fucked him yet?" Liz asked, bluntly as ever. They all laughed, and Melissa shyly shook her head. "Good God girl, get it done!" It didn't take much to get Liz tipsy and the more alcohol she consumed, the more vulgar her sexual innuendos would get.

"Liz!" Melissa laughed; even though she was often taken aback by some of Liz's comments and actions, she loved being in her company and she could not stop giggling at the shocking things she said.

All three ladies were in good spirits and spent the whole time getting ready laughing and suggesting more and more outrageous things for Mel to text Anthony - ones she would never in a million years even dream of sending - neither would they, despite the bravado - it was purely for entertainment purposes.

"Stick the stereo on, Col!" Liz shouted from the kitchen, as she poured more drinks. Colette knelt on the armchair and reached across the sideboard to the stereo. Within a couple of seconds of pressing the power button, the CD was playing, and Colette turned the volume up. "I can't get up my high hopes and I can't let you go, oh no, you are the one who makes me feel soooo real yeah, yeah, yeah!" Liz belted out the lyrics as loud as she could as she danced her way into the living room, precariously balancing three homemade Cosmopolitans in her hands. "There you go, ladies!"

"Cheers!" they all chorused as they clinked the glasses, spilling a bit out of each glass onto the real wooden floor below. They proceeded to each dance around with towels on their heads, wearing their dressing gowns and holding their glasses in the air, taking large gulps in between singing. It was 'Somebody Else's Guy' by Jocelyn Brown that they were each belting out and it had become a staple in the ladies' favourite song lists; whenever it would play, they would flock to the dance floor - the dance floor being the living room's fluffy rug in this instance. It had begun as a symbol of Liz's ongoing facade with her on and off attached boyfriend, and now Melissa found herself relating to every word herself. Mel looked around smiling; she felt so safe when she was with Liz and Colette. They had seen so much more of life than she had and they were opening her eyes to the fact that there was a lot more out there for her than just being Chris's emotional punch bag, or even being with Anthony. They were showing her that one day, when she was ready, she'd be ok no matter what. As they continued dancing, she decided to bite the bullet and message Chris:

TO CHRIS - I MEANT TO TELL YOU IM STAYING OUT TONIGHT AT LIZ'S ITS A WORKS NIGHT OUT. I'LL SEE YOU AFTER YOUR MATCH TOMORROW. GOING OUT THE DOOR IN FIVE SO MIGHT NOT REPLY. NIGHT X

Before she had a chance to receive a reply and allow him to dampen her mood, she switched over the SIM card, (which she had hidden inside her bras for the past few days) and swapped it over into her Nokia phone. Popping her phone into her black patent clutch bag ready for the night ahead, she walked back into the living room. "Right girls, upstairs, time to get our glam on!" Liz ordered, leading the way.

They waited for the taxi and as they were about to head downstairs, Melissa looked into the large full-length mirror that hung on the wall just before the bedroom door, and she looked surprised. 'I do look quite nice actually'. She couldn't remember the last time she had looked at herself that way. Her dress clinched in at her waist and highlighted her curves tastefully. With a sense of empowerment in her stride, she bounced down the stairs after the girls who were already sat in the taxi.

The music was loud in the club, they were having to screech in order to hear each other but they were dancing away shaking their hips and sexily swaying to the beats. They were inundated with random guys approaching them, but there was only one guy on Melissa's mind. Drink by drink, her thoughts strayed to him more and more and her confidence grew. She made her way to the toilets to escape the noise for a moment and to check her phone. As she pulled it from her clutch bag, there was a message from Anthony,

FROM ANTHONY - MISSING TALKING TO YOU, HOPE U R HAVIN A GOOD NIGHT? I BET YOU LOOK GORGEOUS xxxx

Her drunken alter ego messaged back without thought or hesitation,

TO ANTHONY - I DO ACTUALLY. WHY DON'T COME AND SEE FOR YOURSELF. xxx

She knew what would happen if he came; this is where she wasn't naive and she also didn't regret asking him, because she realised, she wanted it to happen.

FROM ANTHONY: ARE YOU SERIOUS? I'D LOVE TO SEE YOU! xxx

TO ANTHONY - YES, I CAN'T WAIT xxx

She fled from the toilets to get the other girls' opinions. Even though he was probably already on his way, she just needed some reassurance that she was doing the right thing. She knew once she crossed this line there was no going back. She would be in the wrong - no matter what Chris and Louisa had done; this would still be wrong. However, there was no hesitation from either Liz or Colette, and they immediately encouraged her,

"YES! Yes, if you want to, of course! You deserve a bit of bloody fun, you're twenty bloody two, for God's sake!" Liz reassured her as she reached into her handbag. "Here, take my spare key, and we'll see you later! One condition though…"

"What's that?" Melissa inquired, accepting the key.

"We want all the gory details later!" They all giggled before exchanging kisses and Melissa reassured them that they didn't need to come outside with her, that Anthony wouldn't be long.

Her heart was pounding with a mix of excitement and nerves as she texted him,

COME AND GET ME NOW, I'VE GOT SOMEWHERE WE CAN GO. DON'T KEEP ME WAITING ITS COLD ;) XXX

FROM ANTHONY - ON MY WAY XXXXXXX

As Melissa waited outside the club, she lit up a cigarette; she didn't feel the cold as much as she did on the way in. The amount of alcohol was obviously providing her with an extra layer of warmth. She couldn't wait to see Anthony and as the headlights of each car approached, the butterflies in her stomach would flutter in anticipation waiting to see if it was him. She wasn't thinking about the consequences. Right there and then she didn't care about the consequences; she wanted him, there was no question now. Maybe it was the face-to-face declaration of love, maybe it was the roses and the meaning behind them or maybe it was just revenge on Chris, she didn't know what it was that made her so sure this was what she wanted. All she knew was that it was what she wanted and nothing was going to change her mind. She continued to drag on her cigarette, with a slight shakiness to her hands as the cold crept in the longer she stood waiting, but then there he was. He pulled over, she smiled cheekily with a hint of coyness. She was completely stepping out of her comfort zone and into unknown territory, but she was drunk. They had had nearly two weeks of foreplay and she felt like she was going to burst. As he wound down his window and flashed his big smile, she melted a little more.

"Get in, Gorgeous," he said with a wink.

Smiling, she ran around the car and opened the passenger door. Her bottom had barely hit the seat before they started kissing, his lips were so perfect and soft, and each kiss was overwrought with passion. He held her body tight, and with each stroke of his hands and brush of his lips she could feel herself falling further; she wanted him there and then. She pulled away, breathless, feeling like she was going to explode at any minute.

"Drive somewhere, quick! Somewhere away from the main road."

Anthony didn't even utter a response before his foot hit the accelerator and they sped off with the sound of the wheel spin echoing behind them. He could barely keep his eyes on the road as Melissa seductively removed her thong. She need not have worried about finding her confidence; she was full to the brim through the mixture of his compliments and the Cosmopolitans she had consumed. He swung his car down a side street and pulled over in front of a row of closed shops, just far enough away so that the streetlight wasn't shining directly into the car - not that by this point they cared anyway- their actions were fuelled with an overpowering lust. They began passionately kissing again as they shimmied through the front seats into the back. Melissa removed Anthony's belt; he was already hard - she couldn't wait for him to touch her, and she felt like she would orgasm as soon as he did. She lay back as they intensely stared into each other's eyes; all the while, with a feather-light touch, he was running his fingers up from her ankle to the inside of her thigh - she let out a gasp as his hand reached in between her legs. Just to tease her, he ran his hand up the other leg instead of touching her intimately, then he lifted her skirt - she let out another gasp, slightly louder than the last. He pulled her towards him, briefly stroking over her clitoris - he could feel she was ready- and he slowly entered her. She felt her head begin to spin and she was breathing fast and deeply. As they became more entwined together and each thrust led them deeper than the last, they groaned in chorus with the rhythmic movements. She was on the edge of euphoria, she could barely breathe; everything about him seemed perfect, the weight of his frame on hers, his smell - just the perfect amount of Issey Miyake, his touch - so soft, his lips - oh his lips, she never wanted them to leave hers. He sensually dragged his lips across her cheeks and proceeded to caress up and down her neck - she sensed the change in the tone of his breathing and consequently heard it echoed in hers. Anthony lifted his head and looked at her with an intense glare. As they drowned in other eyes, the increase in noise from them overwhelmed the car and they came together, an eruption of warmth washed over her entire body and sent shock waves shuddering through her. She had never experienced sex where she came at the same time as her partner -that is if she came at all - and it was a whole other level than what she was used to. Anthony collapsed on her chest, lifting his head again for only a brief second to give her a kiss. They were both covered in a dusting of sweat that glistened when speckles of it hit the distant rays of the streetlight. They lay quietly - aside from their heavy breathing winding down - holding each other like they never wanted to let go. Her chest rose and fell with each recovery breath she took, and he gently kissed the top parts of her breasts that were visible from the cut of her top. It sent shivers down her spine - in a good way.

A few minutes later, they could hear a few people chatting and singing on what seemed like the other side of the road. They began to sit up gradually, checking if the coast was clear. Once the group's voices became more distant, they sat up and laughed as the car was completely steamed up and there were finger marks visible on the rear passenger window - not too dissimilar from the scene in the Titanic film. Melissa caught a glimpse of herself in the rear-view mirror; the passionate encounter had left her pink lipstick smudged around her lips and marks of mascara smudged under her eyes. "I don't look so hot now," she chuckled whilst pointing to her face.

Anthony gently held her chin and with a real sincerity in his tone replied, "You're beautiful," and he leaned in for another long and lingering kiss.

She had never known such warmth and kindness before, during or after any of her sexual encounters, and even though this had just happened on the back seat of a car down a side street, it was the most special sexual experience she had ever had. She felt like she finally got why people raved about 'making love' because that had certainly felt that way.

They clambered back over into the front seats, with Melissa trying her best not to let the cocktails send her flat on her face into the footwell, as she struggled to sexily get back over - and she had so wanted to keep up her new sexy aura going. Once they made it back to their seats -without any embarrassing falls or getting her leg stuck - Anthony enquired, "Where to now?"

Melissa waved Liz's keys at Anthony in a cheeky manner. He winked and started up the car, "Which way?"

Unable to keep their hands off each other, they scrambled their way up the stairs, pulling at each other's clothes as they made their way to Liz's spare room.

The second time was even more incredible than the first, and as they fell out of each other's arms, they just lay on the bed, gazing into each other's eyes. It was like they had a language all of their own; without words, they knew what each other liked and wanted.

After around 20 minutes of kissing and cuddling without a word, they knew Anthony would have to leave soon - not that Liz or Colette would mind him being there or seeing him - more the opposite, in fact, they would have revelled in it and eaten him alive!

He left in just his blazer, bare chest and trousers, as Melissa stood in only his shirt, waving him off, whilst leaning on the half-closed front door.

After he drove off and she shut the door, she waited for the wave of guilt to wash over her - but it didn't. She felt happier than she had ever known. She lay down on the couch, intending to wait up for Liz and Col coming home, but all the adrenaline (and alcohol) must have knocked her out.

She was woken with her senses being teased by the smell of bacon. She opened her eyes and saw Colette sat on the floor, flicking through the T.V channels. She could hear Liz clanging away in the kitchen, humming songs from last night.

"Morning." Melissa yawned as she pushed herself up the couch into a sitting position.

"Good morning lovely!" Colette spoke excitedly with a knowing smile.

Liz popped her head around the door - whilst juggling eggs and bagels just behind, trying not to look chaotic. "Nice shirt," she winked.

Melissa just smiled shyly; she was on a high and she wasn't sure how to come down.

Popping her head back round the door again, "Eh! But I never said you could do it on my couch!"

Liz said with a wink, before disappearing back behind the door.

"We didn't!" Melissa defended with a huge smile.

"Tell us all the details then honey…." Colette sat poised and ready for more information.

"Wait!……. Wait for me…. just one minute..." Liz yelled from the kitchen before dancing excitedly through the kitchen door in a silk leopard print dressing gown, holding two plates and balancing a third on her arm, looking very waitress like! "There!" She handed out their bacon and egg bagels and sat next to Melissa on the couch.

Melissa told them everything, no detail spared, she couldn't help but gush - she was completely besotted.

CHAPTER 8.

A REAL DATE

She was just over three weeks into this crazy affair. It had hit her so fast, like a cold-water shark attack, that she didn't even know she had been hit. She spent most days not knowing whether to laugh or cry at the seriously sticky situation that she had found herself embroiled in. Should she swim against the tide, or just let it sweep her away? She continuously fought with her own conscience and the feelings of guilt she had over it, but at the same time, each day, more and more - she was convinced she was in love with him. It felt as though she had finally found the movie-type love, the type people long to find. It was like he was her Prince Charming and he had come to rescue her from this miserable life she had become trapped in.

She woke every day smiling and no longer worried about whether she would be left alone for another night. Instead, she did things to irritate Chris so that he would argue with her and leave the house sooner than he intended. Some nights, she wouldn't even come home after work, choosing to go to friends for tea just so that she could talk to Anthony - when she knew he wouldn't be with Louisa of course.

It was Friday and Anthony suggested that they go out for the day somewhere on the Saturday. They hadn't seen each other since last weekend and Anthony insisted, he needed to take her out on a 'real' date as he wouldn't normally do things the 'wrong way round'. Louisa was heading to Liverpool that night for a work colleague's hen do and wouldn't be back until Saturday teatime. He suggested they go somewhere for the night at first, but then said he didn't want it to be about sex, that he wanted to wine and dine her like she deserved. Everything he said just oozed romance and she did occasionally catch herself - just for a moment - wondering if he what he was saying was sincere; could he really be that nice? She was secretly relieved though, as she

103

wasn't ready for a premeditated hotel stay. But equally the thought of going out for the day, together, made her feel she was going to spontaneously combust from the nerves and anxiety. That somehow that the day out seemed a lot less severe a thing to explain if they were caught out.

"What if someone sees us, though?" She was discussing her plans with Liz and Colette during their pub lunch. [They always had a pub lunch on a Friday, and they always had an hour for lunch instead of the usual half an hour - even Colette!]

"Come round to mine in the morning; I'll iron your hair and he can wear a cap and Bob's your uncle!" Liz suggested as she clasped her hands with excitement, like she had just solved everything.

"Iron my hair?" Melissa looked puzzled - and a little nervy.

"Oh, come on, Mel, that's what everyone does these days! I'll blow dry it first and then iron it, then no one will recognise you. Oooh, it will be like a role-play day, how exciting!"

They all giggled, and Melissa agreed to Liz's proposal - anything to make her less recognisable.

As Saturday came, she could see the sun beaming through the cracks in the curtains of the bedroom. 'Perfect,' she thought, with a knowing smile. She looked to her side, Chris was still sleeping. His mouth wide open with a gathering of saliva in either corner of his lips. "Uuggghhh," she grimaced, rolling her eyes, then she quickly jumped out of bed and ran to the bathroom. She showered, then put on a fresh pair of pj's and went downstairs, with a towel wrapped around her hair. She put on the television and began to watch the Saturday morning telly. Her tummy was filled with flutters, so she couldn't face breakfast; the cornflakes in her bowl had doubled in size and were starting to disintegrate they'd been there that long. She started to feel a little bit sick. It was as if she was about to find out some exam results or take her driving test again. She was flitting from excitement to fear, from moment to moment. Despite the fact she knew she had already done wrong and she couldn't go back from that, it felt like that by going out today, it would be official. She was having a 'proper' affair – and that, that was forbidden territory she never thought that she would be the type of person to enter, yet now she was here. She could still pull out, yet she didn't want to, she couldn't. No matter how much the voices in her head would try and rouse the good girl inside, there was another voice telling her to follow her heart.

She heard Chris get up, the floorboards creaking as he moved around, along with the sound of slamming drawers. He went into the bathroom to shower, and with that, she left the house as quickly and as quietly as she could, still in her pj's as she had her new date outfit ready at Liz's. She got in her car, switched on the engine, and put the window right down, turning the volume up on her car stereo as she sped off the drive. She felt her happiness beaming out, radiating from her whole body. She had escaped the house and she was about to escape her 'real life' for the day, so she couldn't be happier. She sang along to the songs at the top of her lungs, simply smiling in return to any fellow drivers who'd caught her eye. Her smile and happy energy were infectious. She found herself wondering how something that was supposedly so wrong, make her feel this good? She arrived at Liz's, who of course, being the budding chef, had made a fancy breakfast. "You need to eat lady; we want you to have your wits about you today and really get to know him on a romantic level. It's no good you being drunk every time you meet him - you need to know how you really feel." it sounded very much like the voice of experience. Liz knew all too well how torturous it was to be in a relationship with someone who wasn't available, so she knew the importance of finding out whether it is worth the heartache or not.

After breakfast, Liz got to quickly straightening Melissa's hair. "Put your outfit on first so it doesn't mess your hair up." Mel smiled; she enjoyed Liz giving her advice and semi-ordering her about; she was becoming the big sister she never had! "There! Amazing!" Melissa was pleasantly surprised by the result of ironed hair. With her wild and slightly frizzy curls gone, she looked sleek and polished, and she liked it!

She sprang out of her car once she had parked in the Pay and Display, and she strode towards the bar she was meeting Anthony in with a newfound sexiness and feeling as if she were 10ft tall.

"What are you doing?" A deep voice bellowed at her whilst tapping her on the shoulder.

She turned with her heart racing. "Oh shit," she thought, only for her eyes to meet with Anthony and his beaming smile. "You!!!" she playfully shoved his chest, "You had me all panicky then!"

"Why, you were only walking in town on your own," he chuckled. "You've just come to do a bit of shopping! Anyway, wow! Look at you; I love it!" She was pleased that he approved of her new hairstyle.

He was so calm and composed, and he didn't seem at all fazed by the fact they were about to openly venture out in public together. He scooped her up towards him, his arms around her waist as he pulled her into him closely and they kissed passionately. Although she would normally be the first to mutter 'get a room' under her breath about any couple showing PDAs, Melissa lost all her inhibitions and senses, becoming unaware of her surroundings. Lost in his intoxicating scent, she became immersed in their kiss, (kisses that got better every time). It was only the car screeching around the car park that disrupted their mini rom-com moment. She felt like it was such a cliché, but she struggled to care. Her overwhelming feelings for him had helped her find a little piece of herself again and as the weeks went on, she was beginning to slowly put herself back together.

They headed to get some brunch, although after her big breakfast at Liz's she wasn't that hungry, but she didn't have the heart to tell him. They strolled along, hand in hand - Anthony couldn't take his eyes off her - "Stop it!" Melissa exclaimed coyly, as she wasn't used to such attention. He had made her feel like she was the only woman who was in town that day. They laughed, talked, and continued to hold hands as their food arrived. Anthony tucked into his full English, but Melissa could only push her Eggs Benedict around her plate. However much happiness she felt, there was an uneasiness of the situation - she was enjoying herself but she couldn't fully relax, frequently scanning her eyes around the room to double-check no-one they knew was there.

"Right!" Anthony slammed his knife and fork onto the plate. "I feel like you're not really with me! You do want to be here, don't you?"

"Yes, of course – well, with you I mean. I, I, I don't know, it's almost like when other people are around it feels wrong, like they all know we're having an affair," she whispered the last word, glancing around frantically as she spoke, "but when it's just you and me, well, it sounds soppy but…"

"But what?" Anthony interrupted impatiently.

"It's like none of that matters when it's just us, but I'm just not comfortable here, in this situation, not one bit; I'm sorry."

"OK!" He paused, his face taking on a mischievous look, "Come on!" he instructed, as he jumped up from his chair, throwing a £20 note onto the table and pulling Melissa up from her chair by her hands.

"Where are we going?" Melissa shouted out to Anthony as he ran ahead holding onto her, whizzing her in and out of the bustling crowds.

"You'll see!"

They arrived at the train station, around five minutes later, completely out of breath. They both bent down, clutching their hands onto their knees whilst they caught their breath.

"Not the best idea to run like that straight after a Full English", Anthony laughed and winced at the same time, clutching at his side indicating he was suffering from a stitch. Melissa laughed and affectionately placed her arm on him, forgetting for a moment that they were right in the middle of one of the busiest places that they could be in Manchester.

Anthony looked up. "That looks like a safe bet to me!" Still breathless, Anthony pointed at the board above the platform with around 10 different train destinations on it.

"What does?"

"Leeds! We can get off and get one to Harrogate."

"What?" Melissa didn't even get a response from him before he started making his way to the ticket booth. She smiled in admiration; she loved how impulsive he was, and she knew today would definitely be one to remember.

Having relaxed during the train journey, Melissa and Anthony stepped off the platform hand in hand. As they followed the crowd towards the town, Melissa was taking it all in. It was the little things she loved and appreciated so much – the way he always held her hand, how he always wanted to check she was ok (even if it was a little too much at times), the way he looked at her – gazed at her. The countryside surrounding the little town was so beautiful, as was the weather. Summer had arrived and so they decided to grab some bits from some of the local deli's and have a picnic and avoid the crowds completely.

They found a spot on the side of a little hill, with the bustling town below them. Anthony popped open the Prosecco, then raising the plastic glasses for a toast; "To us and our first proper date." He leaned in for a short but meaningful kiss and they lent on each other's foreheads, gazing into each other's eyes. The air was filled with the sweet aroma of freshly cut grass, the sounds of birds chirping and bees buzzing by provided the perfect soundtrack to their romantic picnic. The scenery was picture perfect, and they lay down peacefully, side by side. Anthony gently stroked her hair away from her forehead and they held hands tightly, letting each other know - without words - that there was nowhere else that either of them would rather be.

The more they sipped on the Prosecco, the more their barriers dropped, and their conversations switched from playful and flirty to deep and meaningful.

"You have leaves again – it's nice." Anthony's random, rather strange statement left Melissa nearly blurting out her Prosecco and half-choking on the bubbles, "Leaves!?" she managed to blurt out with only a slight chuckle escaping. "What on earth do you mean?" she smiled.

"Ha, ha," Anthony blushed looking slightly embarrassed, "I mean I've been watching you these past few years and it's like you have withered away – you know like a tree in the winter – it's there, but looks like it's got no life to it, no leaves."

Melissa realised that his statement, although strange (and slightly funny), was actually quite a sad analogy of her personality and it made her adopt a reflective expression.

"What is it Liss? He asked. Why have you let him do this to you? I remember you were always a right feminist and so feisty, 'anything boys can do, I can do better'," he smiled before his face took on a more serious tone. "I just don't understand what happened? You seemed to come back from Ayia Napa a different girl." Melissa remained silent, just looking back at Anthony, unsure how to address his inquisitive words. "I know you cheated on him with a couple of guys…." he continued. She couldn't get the words out of her head. "But it still doesn't make sense why you came back so different. What was it that happened to you in Ayia Napa Liss?"

As Melissa turned her head away from him, a tear fell from her eye. She felt overwhelmed and cornered by questions that she wasn't sure she was ready to answer.

"Liss! You, ok?" Anthony tried to pull her back to face him, but she brushed him off, looking up at the sky, desperately trying to hold back her tears, "What have I said? What is it?" Anthony's face was fraught with concern.

The statement "you cheated on him" had provoked a reaction from her she couldn't grasp; she didn't want him to think of her like that. "A cheat, it wasn't like that" she thought. It made her sad that he already did, that everybody did. This was the first time *she* had ever cheated. It wasn't like she had made a habit of it, but it was important to her that he knew that. She also quickly realised that if they were ever going to go anywhere in this relationship, she had to trust him with her secret and trust that he would believe her. But then the thought of revisiting that night, that holiday, made her skin crawl and she felt physically sick.

"I didn't cheat, Anthony, it wasn't like that" she blasted. She took a deep breath in anticipation for what would be a tough conversation. She looked him straight in the eye, and placing her heart on her sleeve, she decided she wanted to fully explain exactly what had happened on *that* holiday. She hesitated for a minute and tried to search for some reassurance in his eyes; could she trust him? Would he believe her? Would he ever look at her the same way again? Her heart started to race a little and she began to feel a little light-headed, then she gulped, took a deep breath. She was finally going to tell someone her deepest secret. The shame of which had been slowly killing her inside for years. But she couldn't let it kill this relationship if she wanted it to work, so she knew it was now or never.

CHAPTER 9.

THREE YEARS AGO

As they baked in the sun, the smell of their coconut oil-laden bodies wafted across her nostrils with each wave of the sea breeze. The sound of the waves crashing ashore and the distant sound of music and giggles coming from the nearby beach bar kept the excitement of the upcoming night out going throughout the day. They had decided the sun loungers were a waste of precious drinking money. Choosing instead to lie on the towels on top of the hot sand. Moving only when turning over to make sure they were creating perfect, evenly-tanned bodies. There was an unspoken competitive quest for the best and quickest bronzed bod of their group. But so far, Melissa's first girls' holiday had been everything she envisioned it would be - liberating, freeing, exciting (if a little daunting at times) and non-stop fun; in fact, each day they would push the boundaries, with the almost forceful encouragement of the reps, to create even more crazy life-long memories. They were free to be as reckless as they wanted to be.

Occasionally, Chris crossed Melissa's mind, but she did not want her first girls' holiday to be consumed with worrying about him and how he might feel back at home. They had only been together for 3 months and she had been looking forward to this trip for a year now. So had decided she was not going to be one of those girls who constantly pined after her boyfriend and made sure everyone knew about it. She'd spoken to Louisa about Chris a little, and even she had brushed it off as a non-topic, even though he was her brother, "Listen, you've been with Chris as long as I've been with Anthony, all of two minutes. They knew we had this holiday booked when we got with them, and I'm certainly not wasting my time worrying about whether they are being wet at home worrying what we're up to!" With that, she downed a shot and went off to the dance floor with the biggest of 'woo hoo's'.

There were 8 of them in total on the trip. Melissa and Louisa shared a mutual friend. That was how they ended up going on the trip together, not particularly because they were the best of friends, but they all knew how to have a laugh and they were certainly doing just that! "Well, there is an upside to Chris's sister being here", Melissa stated, turning to Vicki, (her best friend.) "Oh yeah? What's that?" she replied. "Well, when I get back, he won't just have my word for it that nothing happened with anyone, he'll have his sisters too! He is bound to believe her, they are thick as thieves, so I'm wiping it from my brain now. I have felt bad not thinking about him, imagining how I'd feel if I was the one back home. But I'm not! I'm here and I'm sure as hell going to keep enjoying every bloody minute of it!" Melissa laughed. Her and Vicki 'cheered' their ice-cold beers, downed them, and then hand in hand, headed to the beach bar dance floor in their accidentally colour-coordinated bikinis and sarongs.

It was 6 pm and they had long abandoned their beach towels and tanning spots, enticed by the lure of the daytime drinking and dancing in the beach bar, when three of the reps turned up to join them!

"Way hey!" shouted Gary, who was a Geordie, to which each of the girls, another mixed group from Birmingham and a group of lads from Wales echoed back!

All the girls fancied Gary and all the boys wanted to be Gary. "Right then, we've got a challenge for yers!" He raised his hands up to command even more attention and captured them further by flashing his cheeky chappie smile. "We're giving away a free pint for everyone who does a bungee jump right now!! Way hey!" The crowd again echoed the 'way hey'.

"Will you do it with me, Mel? Please? I've always wanted to do one - it will be ace!" Vicki was jumping up and down in front of Melissa with her hands clasped together in a begging gesture. Melissa raised her eyebrows; it wasn't something that had ever appealed to her and for that moment she did wonder how safe a bungee jump run by some reps on an under 30's club holiday would be? But as quick as the thought came into her head, she remembered that she made a promise to herself to do something every day that scared her. "Alright, I could do with another pint!" She replied. They fell about laughing and joined the line of other holidaymakers who were also up for the challenge. Of course, the reps went up first on their own, and Gary, wanting to add his own stamp to it, decided he would, of course, be doing it naked. Strapped to a plastic chair from the bar. Everyone was of course impressed, and he got a chorus of cheers as he stepped up to the plate and throughout the whole performance, as that is exactly what it was - a performance.

Aside from Melissa and Vicki, there was only Marie from their group of friends who was doing it too, only she was doing it with her 'boyfriend' from the Birmingham group (they were 2 days into a full-on holiday romance) and they were up first. As Melissa looked up, she actually felt quite excited watching Marie take the plunge and any nerves she had were slowly disappearing. Vicki, on the other hand, appeared to be changing colour and 'flapping' with dread the closer it got to their turn. "Aww, I'm not sure now Mel, we don't have to do it now if you don't want," she said, looking to Melissa to give her a 'get out of jail free card.' But Melissa knew she would regret it if she didn't do it, they both would, so she wasn't going to let her back out now. "No, don't worry, I'll do it with you, I want that free pint now we've queued for it!"

"Oh, ok!" Vicki looked unimpressed by Melissa's flippancy at the situation.

"Look, Marie's done it! Marie!" Melissa and Vicki waved Marie and her Birmingham boyfriend, Martin, over. "Was it good? What was it like?" Melissa questioned excitedly. "It was brill..." Marie was bursting with pride and eager to describe more when Louisa shouted from the chairs behind them, "What's that on your shoulder? Erggh gross, he's snotted on you!" Lo and behold, there it was for all to see, probably the biggest boggie anyone had ever seen; Martin had in fact 'snotted' on her!

As everyone erupted in laughter, Marie looked at a horrified Martin. "Wipe it off! Wipe it off now!" She marched off with Martin in hot pursuit behind her; it looked like a make-or-break moment in their holiday romance.

As the giggles and jeers continued, Mel and Vic realised it was their turn next.

"Good on you, Baps, I knew you'd be up for it! I bet you are up for anything you!" Gary said, suggestively, towards Melissa. Gary had 'playfully' nicknamed her 'Baps' since the arrival meeting, due to her ample bosom. "Eh, we might get a sneaky peak whilst she's up there, if we're lucky, eh lads!" He gestured further with a wink that was followed with a chorus of cheers from the boys. Melissa rolled her eyes; what others seemed to find charming in Gary, she found quite neanderthal and childish.

He responded to her eye roll by grabbing her hand. "Aw, stop playing hard to get, Baps, and just give us a little flash will ya!"

"Oh yes, no probs, seeing as though you've asked so nicely, of course I will!" Melissa's sarcastic response and further eye rolls prompted further giggles from the crowd of holidaymakers.

"Right ladies, your turn!" Becky, the young girl rep from London was waving her hand for them to join the bungee operator on the crane, as it was their turn to be hoisted up over the cliff and jump off the crane over the sea.

"Oh, fuck!" exclaimed Vicki, who was now completely white. She squeezed Melissa's hand tightly and they made their way over to be strapped in and buckled up together. She couldn't quite take in all the instructions; all she knew was that she and Vicki were now bound together at their feet, they had to hug and jump off the crane at the same time together. 'Simple really,' she thought. As the white rickety crane, that was decorated with a dusting of rust, went further up into the sky. It changed its direction, moving further away hovering over the sea. Right up until everyone below slowly started to look more like a family of ants.

The wind was blowing a lot harder the higher up they got, and it was swinging the crane from side to side slightly making even her slightly nervous now, just for that second.

"Ready?" shouted the Cypriot operator.

They didn't speak, they just looked into each other's eyes with a knowing look and nodded their heads. They shuffled towards the edge of the crane, and as soon as the operator hit the end of the countdown and shouted 'go', they jumped together in sync, leaping from the platform of the crane, freely into the sea air with only a large elasticated rope to bind them, and stop them from plummeting into the sea below. The feeling was that of pure exhilaration, like nothing she had ever known. She felt like she was flying, her body was pumping with adrenaline and her face showcased the biggest of smiles! She let out a scream - not one filled with fear but of pure delight. She could feel Vicki clinging to her with every fibre of her being, but it didn't faze Melissa; she literally felt as free as a bird.

As they reached the ocean, their heads momentarily dipped into the deep blue waters. She knew their thrilling but short journey from the sky was ending, and she had never been more pleased that she had pushed herself to do something. The crane swung them gently back towards the top of the cliff and lowered them onto the mats where the reps were reaching out for them below!

They lay down and now they were on solid ground, it was like Vicki could allow herself to finally enjoy the experience. They couldn't stop giggling. "That was amazing! Where's my pint?" quickly said

Melissa. She, in all seriousness, was in desperate need of a drink, but everyone laughed at the desperation in her tone.

"Grab them their pints, Becky!" shouted Gary, who, like everyone else was laughing at Melissa.

"You should become a rep you, gal" stated Becky, as she handed Melissa her well-earned pint. Melissa laughed it off. "I'm serious, I think you'd be great! Think about it; you don't have to go home then!" Melissa just smiled politely.

They had all stayed at the beach bar until the early hours, dancing the night away with the sand under their feet, absorbing the beats from the DJ and drinking under the stars.

BACK AT THE APARTMENTS

She quenched her thirst with a large fresh orange poured over ice into a plastic pint pot and she sat on the balcony watching the remaining partygoers leaving the pool after jumping in, fully clothed, for a post-club cooldown, or only just returning to the complex to hit their beds. She couldn't believe what a fantastic time she was having; it even crossed her mind that what Becky said about her being rep material could be true. The longer she was there, the more she valued her independence and the thought of being free to travel and do whatever she wanted. It appealed to her much more than the thought of returning home and pursuing the 'safe' route of a relationship with Chris, college, and a Saturday job.

She couldn't help but wonder whether she had genuinely found herself at a crossroad. She pondered as she sat alone, listening to the sounds of crickets and the distance music from the clubs, but equally, she wasn't going to dwell on it. She still had seven days left and she couldn't wait to embrace each and every one! So she went to bed.

The next night, the girls had returned from the beach early for a shower and to get properly dressed up. They were all excited about tonight, as they were hitting the main strip on one of the excursions. It was the biggest night of the holiday, 'The Big Bar Crawl', and they would be hitting all the best bars along the way. The place was heaving; the electric atmosphere was being soaked up with the hoards of teens making the most of every minute of their unsupervised freedom, along with every free shot. After a couple of hours, Melissa sat down at the bar, happily dancing along to the music, in the seat of her stool, she was in a world of her own. She glanced around and realised that two of her friends hadn't come back from the toilet and the other three had gone off with some lads they had met from Southampton.

"Have you seen Vicki and Louisa, or any of the girls?" Melissa shouted above the loud music to Gary, the rep, who was standing behind the bar.

"Yes, they have gone to the Laguna bar," he replied.

Melissa was puzzled; they had all promised they wouldn't leave each other alone, and every night, no matter how inebriated they got, they always made sure they had each other's backs. She thought it was strange that they had just gone without her. It was only around 9pm, so it wasn't even late; she only felt a bit tipsy. "They must have had some shots without me. I bet they're so pissed they've forgotten about me! Charming!" She didn't feel scared as she had known Gary for a week now, and as much as he had not stopped flirting with her, he was a nice guy and the other reps were around the bar rounding everyone up too. "I'll just finish this drink then I'll go and catch them up," she informed Gary. She then proceeded to suck her drink up through her straw quickly so she could get going.

AN HOUR LATER

She slipped in and out of consciousness, fighting to keep her eyelids open so she could try and take in her surroundings; something didn't feel right, she didn't feel right. Blinking slowly, attempting to keep her heavy eyelids from closing yet again, Melissa felt really strange, dazed, the room was pitch black and she couldn't hear a thing, she could only feel the weight of something pressing down on top of her body; the heaviness was making her feel quite breathless. She was completely confused as to where she was and what was happening. As she tried to take in surroundings and make sense of where she was, all that she could make out was a wooden chair and it was upside down, it was then that she realised it wasn't the chair that was upside down, rather it was her head that was upside down. Her eyelids were trying once again to fuse together so she tried to push them back up by rolling her eyes upwards. Her head was hanging off the edge of the bed and her chest tightened. She could only move her eyes, not her arms, not her legs; nothing would move except her eyes. Her body seemed set like cement. Light began to shine into the room. It was coming from an opening door, and it allowed her to take in a little more detail. She realised it was the head rep, Tim, as he walked through the door. She barely had time to compute anything that was happening before she realised, he was naked and walking straight towards her. A pain struck in her chest, her breathlessness increased, her heart began to race, and she wanted to scream, but nothing would come out. She glanced her eyes forward, straining to look past the end of her nose, and she realised the heaviness that she could feel pressing down on her body was Gary. He was laid on top of her, looking right at her, and it was at that moment she knew that he was having sex with her. She tried to force herself to move but she couldn't; she wanted him off her and to escape, but she was frozen to the spot, unable to do anything but watch him carry on. She could not understand what was happening to her; she felt like her breath was running out; it was like she was suffocating. Within moments, she passed out.

The following morning, she awoke feeling groggy. She was naked, sore, and alone. She felt like she had been battered and bruised between her legs. She was in an unfamiliar room. She started trembling as the brief yet devastating memory of last night pained her forehead and a feeling of sickness overwhelmed her. She felt sick to the pit of her stomach with shame and totally lost with confusion. 'I wasn't that drunk, was I? How could I have been so stupid?' she wanted to cry, but she was in total shock, and her tears were stuck in a large lump in her throat. If it wasn't for the physical pain that she was feeling, she would have thought it had just been a nightmare. She wrapped the white sheet off the bed around her and she hesitantly got off the bed. Her face drained of its colour with each small movement and she winced with the searing pain from inside her vagina. She started to tiptoe around the room, trying to locate her clothes, then she spotted them. Chillingly, they were folded neatly on a chair in the corner, the same wooden chair that she had seen last night; she heaved as the memory flashed up again. She discreetly tried to put her clothes on whilst still trying to keep the sheet around her; although no-one was in the room, she felt dirty and exposed and wanted to stay covered. As she got dressed, she noticed a gallery of photography displayed on the bedroom wall, each one stuck by a single piece of sellotape at the top of the photo. She moved towards them to look closer. They were all pictures of girls. Girls who were all asleep (or rather passed out), half-naked, only covered by a white sheet, just like the one she had wrapped around her. Right then, as she studied the images, getting dressed into her clothes from the night before her first tear escaped, she knew something wasn't right about the situation, but she blamed herself; she must have drunk much more than she thought, and she had been irresponsible. A huge lump that had building up in her throat, finally released the sadness that was overwhelming her, and her eyes filled with water, as the reality of what had happened to her began to set in. She felt like the walls were closing in on her, the room started spinning and she just had to get out of there, not that she knew where 'there' was. She leapt towards the door, hurriedly pushing down the handle to open it and she fell into the living area of the apartment - Gary and Tim were sat on the couch in their orange rep shorts and white branded vests, all ready for the day ahead, "Morning!" they chorused, as if nothing had happened. She had never noticed how repulsive they were before. Tim was balding with prominent man boobs and a large beer belly, and Gary – she couldn't even look at him, she had thought he was a nice guy, a friend even, but now all she could see was the smugness that covered his face whilst he was having sex with her, an image she knew would never leave her - ever. He knew she couldn't move; she had seen it in his eyes, it was like he had won. It was like she got what she deserved for rebuffing his advances.

"Mo...morn-ning" she shuddered a reply, feeling extremely uncomfortable being alone in their company, sweat began to drip from her brow, then there was a knock at the door before the person the other side opened it. It was the rep, Becky. "OOOH! Check you out, you saucy minx! I knew you would give in to Gary, they always do!" That comment sent shivers down Melissa's spine, as she pictured the photos of all the girls on his wall. "Ready for the walk of shame back to your apartment?" she cackled, as she put her arm around her and accompanied her out of the door. With each painful step, the memory of Tim entering the room kept flashing into her thoughts. Although she had no memory of him doing anything other than walk into the room, she knew deep down inside what he had come in there for and the internal screams racing through her body kept reinforcing her worst fears. Becky was as chirpy as usual and was chatting away, totally unaware of Melissa's gut wrenching and heart racing, nor did she notice how she kept constantly looking up to stop herself from bursting into tears. She could see Becky's lips moving and muffled sounds coming from them, but she had no clue what she was saying. As they arrived at the apartment block, Melissa felt immense relief; she felt like her legs were going to give way, her lips were quivering as she struggled to keep a lid on her emotions. She left Becky in the lobby saying she desperately needed the toilet, and she frantically dashed off towards her apartment. She was trying to run up the stairs as the tears began streaming, and between her legs

134

burned. She banged on the door as she had no key, and thankfully Vicki answered quickly,

"Hey you, where have..."

"I…I …need the toilet," Melissa forced herself past Vicki, almost pushing her over, and ran to the bathroom locking the door swiftly behind her. She slid down the door onto the cold bathroom floor, she pulled her knees up to her chest, wrapping her arms around them and lay her head down and she started sobbing uncontrollably. Her silent tears turned into a painful howling sound. She felt violated on so many levels and then Chris came into her mind; he would never believe her that she didn't know; that she hadn't meant to, and with those thoughts, she turned to the toilet and began to heave. As she was being sick, Vicki was gently tapping on the door, "Mel, are you ok honey? I can hear you crying, I'm worried about you babe, can I come in?"

Melissa didn't know what to do; she daren't say the words out loud, she didn't even want to say them in her head, nobody would believe her, they would just say she must have got too drunk and had gone back there willingly. "I'm… fine…Vic…I just feel ill…I'll be out in a minute." She desperately tried to compose herself. She slid along the floor on her bottom towards the sink, flinching with every shuffle. She managed to reach up to the sink pulling herself up using the basin; she felt void of all energy and as she dragged herself up, she glared at herself in the mirror. She had reams of watery mascara smeared down her face, she didn't look like she used to - she felt robbed of herself. "You are a stupid, stupid, stupid cow!" she cursed herself through gritted teeth, then she turned away, unable to look at herself any longer.

"Mel, are you coming out babe? It's only me here; talk to me, please?"

Melissa turned to the bathroom door, she opened it and fell into Vicki's arms, she clung to her, and she felt safe for the first time that morning. She closed her eyes tightly shut and longed for the reoccurring visions in her head to disappear.

'BANG, BANG, BANG'

Melissa jumped out of her skin, "Who the hell's this?" exclaimed Vicki. She headed out the bedroom toward the apartment front door, as Melissa slumped onto one of the beds.

"YOU SLAG!" Louisa barged into the bedroom. Melissa didn't even look up. "You got nothing to say for yourself? Eh! Look at the state of you, you tramp. Everyone is talking about you downstairs. Oh, and don't worry, I've already phoned Chris for you, and filled him in on your filthy threesome, so don't bother phoning him, he said to say you're finished!"

"Alright, Louisa, that's enough!" Vicki was unnerved by Melissa's behaviour, lack of fight and even emotion so she started pulling Louisa out of the bedroom door. Melissa could hear them bickering, but she wasn't really there; she felt so out of sorts and shaken, she wasn't sure she would ever feel the same again.

The remaining seven days of the holiday were vastly different from the first. She pretended she had a cold for the first few nights, as she just couldn't face going out. Vicki tried her best to provide comfort, but Melissa was in a zombie-like state and although she appreciated Vicki's efforts, she couldn't find comfort in anything she said. After three nights hiding away in the apartment, she decided she couldn't just shut herself off from the world forever and that it was time to just face everyone, regardless of their opinions and how much they may be judging her.

She desperately tried to put a front on, but the first night out was hard, really hard. Despite the fact that the majority of their group didn't seem to have any opinion on her 'threesome' whatsoever, she was a world away from the bubbly girl that she had been 4 days ago. There was, of course, one person who most definitely had an opinion on the situation - Louisa, and she spent the whole night making it clear by burning holes in Melissa with her eyes. Deflated, Melissa seemed to zone out, staring eerily into space. Vicki noticed, and said, "Mel, please don't worry about Louisa, the only reason she's behaving like this is because she's jealous, she wanted to cop off with Gary herself and she's been fuming since the start of the holiday that he fancied you and not her." Melissa turned to Vicki to acknowledge that she was listening to her, but she had no words. If only Louisa knew what had really happened and the emotional turmoil that she was going through, then she would soon realise that she had absolutely nothing to be jealous about. "Do you want another drink?" Vicki asked. Melissa shook her head, "No thanks, Vic, I'm ok with this one for now, thanks though". As Vicki walked towards the bar, Melissa took a swig from her glass, it was lemonade and she had pretended it was vodka and lemonade all night. Only buying drinks for herself in order not to draw attention to the fact that she wasn't drinking as she couldn't handle the questions. There was no way that she was going to do anything that made her even the slightest bit vulnerable or out of control. As the night went on, the girls headed to the club and straight to the dance floor, Melissa plastered on a smile and went through the motions. She had always loved dancing, but it was like she couldn't hear the music anymore or feel it in her soul like she used to. She felt nothing inside.

The next day, as the girls lounged around the pool, Melissa and Vicki sat at the poolside bar, perched on their stools. They both were sat there wearing, unintentionally, matching denim skirts and identical purple bikinis. They were chatting about anything and everything they could, completely avoiding what had happened the other night - Melissa knew the only option she had was to completely block it out, in order for her to try and move on. Eventually, Vicki said something that made her laugh, and as she giggled away. she felt her troubles start to dissolve a little. She started to feel relaxed and happy in that moment for the first time since the other night. Suddenly she was startled by something, or rather someone, going up the back of her skirt. She jumped and her mind began racing as she spun around on the stool, only to be greeted by "let me know when you're ready for round two, Baps!" Gary arrogantly quipped with a wink, before walking away chuckling to himself. Melissa's stomach turned, Vicki looked stunned and unsure of what to do. As Melissa's nausea built up, she yearned for the holiday to be over; another 2 days in this place seemed like a lifetime, so she needed to escape this nightmare and go home.

Vicki told her in a knowing way how she knew Melissa had been 'set up' *that* night. "When we'd left the toilets that night, it was Tim told me that you'd said to meet us at the Laguna bar!" (Leaving Melissa alone in the bar with Gary, as they'd obviously planned beforehand.)

When she returned to the U.K., more torturous moments lay ahead though, as she had to go and have STI and HIV tests at the local clinic. She felt broken inside and unsure of how to put the pieces of herself back together. Sick to the pit of her stomach, replaying the little memories she had over and over in her head, each time they played out she could physically feel the weight of his heavy body on hers. She would try to mentally push him off, but she couldn't; she also tried to scramble to the door to shut Tim out each time she re-lived him entering the room, but she couldn't. She just had to watch it and feel it all over again and again. Tortured and tormented, she knew something wasn't right but what could she say? She was drunk, she was a fool, she was an idiot, as if anyone would think anything otherwise. Waves of nausea continually swept over her body; she had barely eaten anything in the weeks since returning home and had already lost nearly a stone in weight; she looked gaunt and weary. She waited alone in that waiting room, just wondering which of the passing nurses or doctors it would be that would tell her that her life was over, that she had HIV. There was no way that Gary and Tim had done this to as many girls as were pictured on that wall without one of them catching HIV, no way, she had read all the dangers about having unprotected sex and it was something she'd never done, yet here she was. She could feel everyone's eyes burning holes in her; she was certain they all knew; they were all judging her, thinking what a tart she was, just like everyone would when they knew. Then thoughts of her family flashed across her mind and the tears flowed freely down her cheeks. She couldn't stop no matter who was watching, she cried because, rather than the shame of telling her family, she knew she would have to take the other unthinkable way out. There was no way that she could tell them what she'd done, how irresponsible she'd been, there was just no way that she could face it.

She had been overwhelmed and numb ever since it happened, not knowing what direction to take, that's why going back to Chris seemed like the only solution. The problem was she had never really processed what had happened, not for months after it happened. When she had returned home from Cyprus, she never confided in anyone else. And Vicki, the only one who did know, moved to London as soon as they got back, as she had a place at King's College on a fantastic course in Health Sciences. Melissa was pleased for her of course, but the timing couldn't have been worse. No one else knew the anguish that she was feeling, the confusion she endured at the sexual health clinic whilst waiting for the HIV results. But the anguish slightly diminished when she found out she was all clear.

She hid away in her bedroom most of the time and bunked off college for a full two weeks before she could face going back. Her dad simply thought she was wiped out from all the partying and then believed her story about college giving them time off for revision, even though the term had just started.

Chris asked to meet her a couple of weeks after they got back and stated he would forgive her betrayal and that he would 'look after' her from now on to make sure that she was never that stupid ever again. As she hadn't even forgiven herself at this point, she was grateful for his forgiveness and began to do whatever he wanted. It was only a year later, when she read an article in Cosmopolitan about date rape, that it became all too clear what had happened to her, but by then it was already too late. Chris held Melissa firmly in his clutches, he had chipped away at her mind, until she barely had one of her own, he rarely let her drink out of the house, he had influence over her clothes, her behaviour, her friends, everything. She didn't see it as anything other than him being protective; it was so gradual that she wasn't even fully aware that he now controlled almost everything that she did.

CHAPTER 10.

PRESENT DAY

Once she had finished talking, Anthony looked shocked; the silence was deafening, as she waited for the judgement from him, for him to change towards her, but instead, Anthony hugged her tightly. She could feel the reassurance and love from him, and she felt like she never wanted to let go. She felt safe, protected and in a way, it was like she had been set free. She could see it in his eyes that he wasn't judging her, that he just wanted to reassure her, and he did. Carrying the secret around with her had weighed her down for years, consumed by the shame, fear and guilt of what had happened but it had gotten her nowhere. Now she had got what she had longed for, for years, to feel reassured, to feel loved and not judged. For someone to just tell her it would all be ok.

"I can't believe Louisa treated you like that! She was meant to be your friend!" Anthony's tone was filled with anger.

"Anthony you can't blame Louisa, she didn't know... I mean, I didn't even know myself at the time, well not properly, anyway. There was no proof. Put yourself in her shoes; I was just a silly drunk slapper who had just cheated on her brother with the 'sexy' rep." Melissa found herself reassuring Anthony, as he ripped up the grass angrily. She stroked his cheek with her hand and lifted his chin, so his eyes met hers. "I don't blame Louisa, or even Chris, so please don't let any anger overwhelm you; there's no point, I should know."

Now, in telling Anthony what she feared telling him most, she felt a new-found strength inside, which reminded her of how she used to feel. Memories of the independent young lady who boarded that plane all those years ago came flooding back. The dreamer, the happy-go-lucky girl, who despite tough times before like the breakdown of her family, she was still full of hope and positivity. In that moment, it was like a lightbulb went off in her head. She couldn't keep dragging around this guilt and shame, letting it eat away at her every day; she couldn't let this define her any longer and she couldn't let Chris continue to treat her like he had been because of it. It was time to plan her escape route - starting today!

"You're smiling? How…" Melissa placed her finger on Anthony's lips to stop him talking and leaned in to kiss him. They kissed softly, prolonged, and meaningful kisses, ones that made her heart flutter slightly. She had such physical responses to kissing and hugging him that she was beginning to see this was more than just lust.

Anthony pulled away for a moment, and looked into her eyes, "Seriously, are you ok?"

"Yes, it's ok. I've just realised that I am actually ok!" Melissa made her first bold affirmation with another smile, and she meant it, she did feel completely ok for the first time in a long time.

Seeing as though she had shared her deepest secret with him, she felt it was only right to ask him something that she had been wondering, "So, why do you put up with Louisa?" (Not noticing the irony in her question.) "Even from the start she would openly flirt with guys right in front you, even kiss them and humiliate you in front of us all. I don't get that, I never did, why do *you* stay?"

Anthony went to speak and then hesitated like he was holding something back, then after a moment he began to open up, "It was being part of the family, such a big family, instantly, and the friends – I always felt welcome."

She understood completely what he meant; it was so hard when her family broke up and it was nice to feel a part of another family, it was like an escapism into another world, since they seemed to be such a big, happy, successful family. It was only with time she had begun to see just how messed up some of its members actually were, although she never knew why they were messed up. Melissa could usually always see reasons behind people's behaviours - she was quite the amateur psychologist after studying it for a year at college. She felt they were harbouring their own secrets.

"But you have a family, a good family, don't you? And they're only around the corner – do you not feel at home there?"

As she asked the question and she saw the struggle in his face, she retrieved memories of how quickly he had more or less, moved into Louisa's bedroom, staying over every night after only a matter of days.

She could tell he was struggling to answer, and she quickly realised this must be something that ran quite deeply. "You don't have to tell me if you don't want to, it's ok."

However Anthony took a long breath and reluctantly began to divulge. "I know my mum loves me, she does, but some days she can barely look at me, so I prefer to stay away to make it easier for her to forget. It's not her fault, it's just because it's too hard."

Melissa took hold of his hand, seeing his eyes fill with tears and placed her other arm around him.

"It's ok," she whispered reassuringly as she stroked his back. She didn't know what he meant or what he was going to say, but after his response to her secret she knew, no matter what, it would be ok if they tackled it together. That thought also made her realise that she wasn't just having an affair, that this was more than that, they were an 'us,' and a 'we', they were *together*.

"My dad, you see, he's not my real dad and my brother and sister are my half brother and sister. My real dad died when I was 3."

Tears fell from Anthony's eyes, and he swiftly wiped each one away with his fingers; as sensitive as Anthony was, it became clear that he was uncomfortable with showing such emotion. Melissa was totally taken aback by what he had said and how raw everything was to him. `How could no one know this?' she thought, then she wondered if he'd shared this with anyone else? Did Louisa know this, had he shared this with her? She thought about asking but then she decided she didn't want to look insensitive or jealous at such a pinnacle moment by bringing up Louisa.

"Oh, I'm so sorry Anthony, I didn't realise. But surely your mum must be so proud when she looks at you; you're lovely – why would you think she can't look at you?"

"I look just like him – my real dad – and my personality is so similar, well, so my Nana says all the time. Of course, I don't remember, and Mum finds it too painful to talk about, so she has never spoken to me about it." He paused poignantly, "It's harder for my mum; they had fallen out, I think it was over money, my dad had lost his job again, he was acting all weird, the way my Nana tells it, it sounds to me like he had depression. They were on the verge of splitting up as my mum couldn't cope anymore; she blamed him and he killed himself, now she blames herself and that's why she can't look at me. I can see it in her face every time she talks to me."

More tears, this time without any attempt to stop them. Melissa said nothing, knowing that sometimes that is best thing to do. After all, what could she say that would help? She felt so much sympathy towards him but knew there are no words.

151

He nestled his head against her chest, and she stroked his hair to comfort him.

Within an hour, their relationship had moved up another level.

CHAPTER 11.

BOOTY CALL

When she returned from that holiday and Chris had asked to meet her, she had tried to explain things to him, about how she felt that something just felt wrong about the whole situation and that she didn't believe she was *that* drunk. She hadn't even wanted to get back with him that night she met with him; it was more a case that, for her own peace of mind she just needed him to know that what he thought had happened simply wasn't the case, that it wasn't her fault. However, her attempts at talking to him fell on deaf ears and for the next 3 years he assured her that it was her fault and that she had brought it on herself. Chris reiterated that he had told her before that she was too friendly with men and that it had only been a matter of time before something like that would happen. The perfect justification for saying that's why he hated her drinking. Although he had always hated her drinking anyway, as he rarely drank due to his strict training regimes. Over the years though, he had become more and more obsessive and controlling of what she could and couldn't drink. She conformed at first, believing every word he said, and in the end, she did it in secret or did as she was told for fear of the repercussions. His so-called forgiveness was the beginning of the end of any equality, if there was ever to be any within their relationship. Every time she said or did anything he didn't like or approve of, she would have to listen to how he had forgiven her, had she forgotten that? Didn't she realise how lucky she was and that no other man would want a dirty slag that had slept with two guys at once? Chris barely let Mel have nights out with friends, (let alone visit Vicki in London; in fact, she had now completed her 3-year uni course and Melissa hadn't even seen her once); now, night's out were few and far between and he had something to say about each and every one of her friends, all which pretty much amounted to the same thing. They were all tarts who were a bad influence on her. So for three years, she was brainwashed and completely compliant. She was a 'Stepford wife' in every sense. The last 6 months, however, saw fate play a hand in her future and after her previous employer had closed down. It forced her to get a new job and the new job, of course, led her to meet Liz and Colette. For the past month, since Anthony became a part of her life in a new way, Melissa was starting to feel more and more rebellious. Her confidence grew and she cared less and less what people thought. She could now see a clear way out and had a real realisation that she could have a life without Chris. She had opened a savings account and registered it at her dad's address so that no statements would come through the door at home. She wanted to start building an exit fund so she was putting as much as she could in. She knew that when the time came, getting any money from the house would be no easy battle. So she had to have a plan B. She organised an afternoon drinking in Manchester with her friend Andie. She didn't even inform Chris of her plans, nor did she have any intention of doing so. He was going to watch United with his dad and it's not like he'd be rushing home, nonetheless, she couldn't care. Melissa was putting on her makeup, dancing in her chair at the dressing table. Old school Whitney Houston blasted out – 'I wanna dance with somebody' - and thoughts of Anthony raced through her mind, followed by the usual heart flutters. She smiled to herself in the mirror before singing into her hairbrush, reenacting a pop video in the mirror.

BEEP BEEP – BEEP BEEP. Melissa turned to her phone.

FROM ANDIE- HEY Gorgeous lady – I'll be getting off the train in town at 6.30, meet me at Piccadilly! Xxx

TO ANDIE - Can't wait!! See you then ☺ xxx

Melissa couldn't wait for a long overdue catch up with her friend Andie - Andrea – but she hated that! Andie insisted she was far too cool for the name Andrea, and she despised it when people called her it. Melissa was so ready for a night out with Andie, because of all her friends, she had the most infectious happy energy. Andie was 17 years older than her, but you would never have guessed. She was stunning looking with immaculate

Caribbean skin- 'Black don't crack', she would always say with a laugh and a radiant personality full of kindness, quick wit and bubbling over with fun. Andie lived on the outskirts of Liverpool, so they didn't see each other much these days, but when they did, they had a ball!

They had met at university when Andie was a mature student –technically, although she was only 29 at the time - now 32 – and Melissa took to her instantly – they just clicked. She admired how comfortable Andie was in own skin, owning her personality and not giving a second thought to anything she said. Neither of them actually graduated from university; it was a historical joke between them how they had failed at the end of the first year after spending too much time in the pub instead of in the library. Under her young and funky exterior, Andie would always have some words of wisdom that would remind Melissa that she had a lot more life experience than she did, and usually she always took what she said on board.

Andie had always loved the champagne lifestyle, but she had always had to improvise a little, as her budget was better suited to lemonade lifestyle instead. She always looked completely fabulous, revealing the secret was to scour the charity shops in the affluent areas nearby for the cast-offs from the wealthy Cheshire WAGS. Melissa liked the idea, but her OCD restrained her from even entering a charity shop, never mind wearing clothes from there – even after 6 washes! But they do say good things come to those who wait, and this is exactly what happened to Andie, and Melissa couldn't think of anyone who deserved it more. You see, Andie had a long-term partner (who always refused to marry her despite them having two children together), and he had cheated on her – not for the first time, or at least she had always suspected. Although she never had any solid proof. However this time he had gone and got another woman pregnant –and you do not get much more in the way of proof than that! Although she was ever so slightly devastated at the time (and rightly so) – he was now fast approaching 40 and finding himself knee-deep in nappies, where Andie was living life to the full, drinking champagne (not Cava anymore, oh no, the real thing), by the bucket load in a massive, detached house on the Liverpool/Cheshire border.

She lived with her teenage and ever-growing independent children, and the man she shares this with, who not only turned out to be rich, but more importantly, the love of her life. Melissa hadn't seen her since the wedding. She couldn't wait to hear all about her fabulous new life. She knew she would end up telling her about Anthony. She could tell Andie anything, especially knowing that she had never taken to Chris either. She guessed her reaction would be similar to that of Liz and Colette.

They met at the train station as planned and as predicted, it wasn't long before everything came flooding out. Pretty much straight after taking their seats, she ended up telling her everything about the whirlwind affair - much to Andie's entertainment. Although she had been on the receiving end of the betrayal of an affair herself, she knew the situation and it was totally different in her eyes. There were no children involved in this scenario, unlike in her's, and she had always treated her other half so well; Chris, on the other hand, didn't deserve her beautiful friend in Andie's eyes and therefore, anything that helped Melissa to see that for herself was ok with her.

"NOOOO! Not that Anthony, you're joking!! That one fancies himself as a cross between David Beckham and Peter André – oh lovey, I think we can do a little better than that!"

Melissa giggled, "He's nice really; admittedly he is a little cheesy, but it's in a nice way!"

"Err huh, if you say so girl!" The way Andie said things tickled Melissa; she had so much expression on her face and tone, not to mention that her parents were from Jamaica, so she would occasionally throw in a Jamaican accent for extra entertainment.

"Well, flipping heck! Old trout mouth won't be happy!" they both fell about laughing. Louisa (old trout mouth) – always a chaperone/spy for Chris - had been out on at least two of Melissa's birthdays when Andie had also been out, and like Chris, she hadn't been keen on her either.

"Well, I never got it anyway girl, I mean your man has got less personality than a wet fish – I mean a dead fish! I think all he's ever said to me was 'UG'." Acting this out with a caveman expression, she had Chris spot on. Why had Melissa ever seen it as an endearing shyness when it seemed obvious that to many people, he was clearly ignorant – not to mention dull? She wondered how she could have been so naive and blind to it.

Andie's energy was infectious; although she was often a little cheeky about others and she didn't mince her words, her heart was that of pure gold and once you had a place there, she would cherish you forever. Melissa just loved their get-togethers; it didn't matter how much time had passed; it was like they had only seen each other yesterday. They supped bubbly like it was going out of fashion – always with a firm 'no to water on the table with the meal' rule. They put the world to rights and had a blast dancing like no one was watching.

Melissa glanced at her phone.

"Is that him now? Well, bloody hell! He can't leave you alone girl!" The Jamaican twang had them giggling again. "Well, at least your smiling girl – *even though you are a bit of a hussy*! No surprise though, living with that sour face!" Andie finished her sentence with a sour face impression and a large swig of champagne.

The pair giggled away, and Melissa read her message.

FROM ANTHONY - I HOPE U R HAVIN A GR8 NITE, I'M GOING 2 STAY AT MY MUMS TONITE SO I CAN MEET U EVEN IF IT'S JUST FOR A QUICK KISS, I MISS YOU. XX

She couldn't contain her beaming smile.

"Well, girl, what does he want? As if I can't guess, hmmm!" She pursed her lips and then smiled with a wink.

"Not that! He just misses me and says he wouldn't mind meeting after."

"He misses your booty, so he's giving you a booty call!" Andie raised her eyebrows and went in for another swig of champagne. "Tell him you'll let him know later because this is a girls' night and we ain't cutting it short for no one, not even a David Beckham wannabe."

"Of course! I promise I won't do that!" Melissa protested. In reality, she knew she had cut far too many girls' nights short because of Chris and his demands. This relationship was going to be different; she wanted to make it clear from the start to Anthony that her friends meant a lot to her, that they had been her only light in all the darkness over the years and she wouldn't be ditching them for anyone.

They had been out since 2pm, had drunk more bottles of champagne than either of them could remember and stood out a mile lapping up the attention after being the first and only people on the dance floor from 6 till 8 pm. When some others joined the dance floor, they then decided it was time for a little sit-down and a few more drinks, seeing as they had probably sweated at least one bottle out of their system.

"I'll get these Andie, you've bought the champagne all night!" Melissa instructed.

"Yeah, well bird, see nowadays I can afford it and I'd much rather you pop that into your getaway fund, ok?" Although she was drunk, Melissa knew that there was no point in protesting as it would only be a waste of time, so she simply embraced Andie tightly and said "Thank you! I really do appreciate!"

"Don't mention it, my girl, honestly, it's nothing!
"

With that, she waved her arms at the barman and managed to get his attention and get served! "Still got it, girl!" she winked at Melissa, proud of the fact she had managed to grab the barman's attention and get served straight away, despite the fact the bar was so busy.

"Andie, what time is the train that you need to get on?"

"Oh yeah, organising your booty call, are you?"

"No! I'm not," she blushed, "ok I am! I'm not cutting our night short though, I would never do that! I'm just arranging to meet him at the train station because I've missed him."

"Oohhh! Girl's got it bad!! Well, as long as you ain't binning me off, I don't care what you get up to, my friend, it's about time that you had a bit more happiness in your life. You're only bloody twenty-two, for goodness' sake, plus your twenties are the years you're meant to make mistakes."

Melissa knew that Andie wasn't trying to discourage her, but she knew she had dropped in the word mistake for a reason. Melissa pondered for a moment; was she making a mistake? Then she quickly shook off any doubt; she knew that she and Anthony was the real deal, and she also knew that once Andie had met him properly and seen them together, then she would know that as well.

The last train back to Liverpool was at 10:55 pm. Andie and Melissa exchanged a prolonged squeeze on the platform.

"Enjoy your booty call!"

"He's just going to take me home!" Melissa insisted, although she wasn't very convincing as Anthony had already suggested that they have at least one drink out together and even if they didn't, she knew that him 'just taking her home' would be likely to involve a lust-filled pitstop somewhere, at the very least.

"I believe you girl, thousands wouldn't!" Andie said with probably her tenth wink of the day, before kissing her goodbye - with a double kiss of course!

"See you, Andie, love you!"

"Love you more, girl, don't you forget it!" Even after a few drinks (well more like a colossal number of drinks), Melissa knew that was Andie's way of making sure she knew that, if by playing with fire the way she was meant that she got burnt, then she would be there for her. Only on rare occasions when Andie showed a little of her 'I'm older and wiser' head, did the age gap ever become apparent. Melissa knew she wasn't patronising her though; it was only because she cared. Although she was worried about things going sour with Anthony, it was reassuring to know that should Chris find out, then she had a place to escape to, albeit for even one night - Andie had a family and Melissa never would have caused the upheaval for them all by going to stay there long-term.

They waved at each other frantically like two giddy schoolgirls, knowing that it would be at least 6 months at the least before their busy schedules would allow them to meet up again. The sound of the train doors beeping echoed all around the quiet station before the doors closed and the train pulled away from the platform. Just like every time she said goodbye to Andie, Melissa felt a pang of sadness; she wished she lived nearer so that they could see each other more. She looked down at her phone. It was 10:57 pm; she better make her way downstairs to the train station entrance in order to meet Anthony. She couldn't wait to see him, and the sadness of Andie's departure was quickly replaced with butterflies at the thought of seeing Anthony any moment. Just as she was about to turn around, "Hey Sexy!" said a deep voice and two arms wrapped around her waist, she almost leapt out of her skin. She didn't recognise the voice; she turned around, startled, unsure as to what she would do when she came face-to-face with what was most likely to be an excitable drunk. Just as she was turning around, the familiar scent of Anthony's aftershave hit her, and she smiled before playfully slapping him.

"Why do you always do that?"

"What?" he replied with his Prince Charming smile flashing with full force.

"Make me jump!"

"You mean make your heart race?" Anthony suggested seductively, before leaning in for a kiss.

"Yeah, well, that too," she grinned from ear to ear as she reciprocated his advances.

The kiss soon became very steamy, and they were most definitely stepping over the acceptable levels of PDAs. The pair of them had obviously become completely unaware of their surroundings. Only the sound of another train pulling in and a stumbling drunk barging into them pulled them out of their moment. Slightly embarrassed, they both started laughing. Anthony followed up their giggles with another fleeting yet meaningful kiss. Even though it was officially summer and the day itself had been quite warm, the temperature had begun to drop, and Melissa shuddered as the chill in the air started to set in.

"Come on, let's go get a drink," Anthony suggested, whilst opening up his jacket, gesturing for her to snuggle up inside it with him.

"Are you sure that's a good idea? Going for a drink? What if someone sees us, Ant?"

"What if? Someone could have already seen us just then! Anyway, if I've got you, I don't care who sees and finds out what."

The air might have been chilly, but she certainly felt all warm inside.

They decided to go to the Triangle Club as it had an outside bit at the back, and they knew it was likely to be quiet at this time of night as most people would be inside dancing. Melissa waited outside wearing Anthony's jacket whilst he went to get them some drinks, not that she needed any more bubbles today if truth be told. She opened her handbag and pulled out a compact so that she could secretly check her makeup before Anthony got back. After doing a couple of quick touch-ups, she checked her phone to see if Andie had texted to say she was home, although it was possibly still a little early for her to be back yet. There wasn't a message from Andie, but there was a message.

FROM CHRIS: WHERE R U? SHOULDNT YOU BE GETTING BACK NOW? I'LL COME AND GET YOU X

She rolled her eyes and put the phone back in her bag without replying. She wasn't going to let him spoil her fun, so she quickly wiped any thought of him from her mind. Just as she was putting her phone back in her bag, Anthony walked around the corner with two drinks and one dashing smile. 'God, I love that smile,' she thought.

"Have I ever told you how gorgeous you are?"

"Maybe once or twice, but you can tell me again if you like?" Melissa replied coyly; she loved how special he made her feel.

They sat and chatted, the thumping sound of the base of the music was all they could hear along with indistinct chatter in the distance. The air was cool but not cold, and the sky was clear and covered in glittering stars that weren't often visible in the city centre. They were right about the beer garden being quiet - they were the only two sat there, huddled as closely as they could be. Their legs were positioned in a way that they were entwined with one another in order to be as close together as possible. Their hands were amorously stroking each other's legs and they were leaned right into each other, resting on each other's foreheads, kissing between sentences. They weren't talking about anything in particular or anything important, merely whispering flirty exchanges in the main, that were raising their body temperatures with each flirty remark.

Anthony moved his hands up the front of her thighs, moving them slowly up and over her hips so that his hands were no longer visible, they were hidden from sight inside of her jacket. He followed her silhouette, moving his hand up to her waist. Her nipples became visibly hard - and it wasn't from the crisp night air.

"Ant, stop, we can't, not here!" she said, her breath getting heavier as the passion started to spill out of them.

He gently held the back of her head, kissed her, leaving her even further breathless and he caressed her neck and collarbone, grazing the top of her cleavage. She was more than aware of her surroundings, but she couldn't help but succumb to his erotic advances. She wanted him, she knew, and he knew it. With each stroke, kiss, the fear of someone seeing them was melting away and they became lost in their own universe. He slowly moved his hands up the inside of her thighs, brushing over her thin lace briefs and teasing her crotch. She let out a gasp and returned the teasing touches and cupping his crotch. Anthony groaned as they continued kissing. They both knew they couldn't go any further where they were. "Come on!" Anthony got up whilst continuing to kiss Melissa and adjusted the growing bulge in his pants. They walked with difficulty whilst remaining locked at the lips; Melissa was unsure as to where Anthony was leading her, but she didn't really care other than hoping it was somewhere in which they could be together properly.

"We'll go to my car; we'll go get a hotel. You can say that you're staying at Andie's."

"OK," she replied, without thinking about it for even a second, as a flurry of butterflies danced in her stomach. The risk stakes were high, a hotel stay was new territory, and for a moment she wondered if her nerves could take it, then the next thought was the idea of waking up in Anthony's arms which made her feel fuzzy inside. She smiled at the thought of it and the feelings it gave her. Just as they got to the club's back door, continuing to kiss, Anthony pressed her up against the wall as he sensually kissed her up and down her neck, her collarbone and her breasts, and Melissa moaned as the pleasure intensified. "Let's go, now, come on!" she groaned, unable to wait any longer.

They had to go through the club to get back out. Within a moment of entering the club, it felt like those butterflies inside her were dancing on her bladder. "Ant, wait, I just need the toilet first," she said, and she danced a little jig to stress the importance that she go right now.

"OK, I'll wait here, but hurry!" he instructed with a sensuous smile.

She danced her way to the toilet; the music was so good, she felt amazing, and she still had the dancing bug following her and Andie's afternoon. She smiled to herself and became lost in her own world as she squeezed through the crowds to get to the toilets. Just as she was about to head through the door to the ladies' toilets, she felt a hand squeeze her shoulder. It immediately pulled her out of her own world and back into the club.

"Hey, you're Chris Clancy's Mrs, aren't you?"

Melissa's eyes bulged a little, her mouth twisted as she wondered how to respond.

"I'm one of his teammates. I've seen you at the games," he leaned over, shouting into her ear over the loud music. She knew who he was, hence, why she was lost for words, "Yes hi! I'm sorry, I just really need the loo!"

"Yeah, course, it's mad actually; I saw him at the game with his old man this afternoon, and I told him to join me for a few beers after."

"What, here?!" she sputtered out the words as her mouth began to get dry and her throat felt like it closed a little.

"Yeah, told him to come here, I'm out with the boys."

"Aw, that's nice, anyway, sorry, really got to dash!" she goofily responded with a further "I need a wee" jiggling, in order to escape. She didn't give him time to say goodbye, she just ran through the door to the ladies, as another guest was going through it. There was a small queue to the toilets;

the longer she stood in it, the longer she felt that both her bladder and brain would literally burst. 'What if he's here now? What if he's sees Anthony and then me?' her thoughts were spiralling. "Oh shit!" she gasped. The other ladies turned around, only to see that she was talking to herself, before throwing her a funny look, to which she responded with an awkward smile. 'What if he's already seen us?' the conversation in her mind began again. "Oh SHIT!" she repeated, only it was louder this time; the funny looks from the other ladies and the returning awkward smile were also repeated. She scrambled her hand around in her bag, her heart was thumping louder than the base of the music and she pulled out her phone.

3 MISSED CALLS FROM CHRIS

FROM CHRIS - I'M COMING TO TOWN TO MEET THE LADS UNTIL U R READY TO COME HOME.X

FROM CHRIS - WHY R U IGNORING ME U SILLY COW?

"OH SHIT!!!" The loudest Oh Shit of them all came out, although this time, she didn't see or respond to the reactions of any others, and she ran her trembling hand through her hair, pulling at it slightly as varying scenarios crashed around her mind. She tried to call Anthony, but there was no time to switch her phone over to the other SIM card. It just went straight to his answerphone. One of the toilet cubicles became available and she dashed in, slamming the door behind her and ringing Anthony again. There was no sound. "Oh, come on!" she directed her words towards the phone that she was shaking at the side of her head before it again went to answerphone. "Noooo! For Fuck's Sake!" she grabbed some toilet roll and flushed the toilet, holding the handle with the tissue before opening the door with it too – (even in such situations and alcohol-induced states, her fear of public toilets and the germs took precedence.) She barged out the door, frantically texting Anthony as she danced her way back through the crowds, scanning the room for any sightings of Chris at the same time.

TO ANTHONY - CHRIS HERE OR ON WAY U NEED TO GET OUT NOW! XX

Despite sending the text, she was still trying to rush back to Anthony to warn him, unsure as to whether he would have seen the text anyway due to his obvious lack of signal. Rushing hurriedly through the crowds, she got knocked off her feet a little by a muscular guy who was rushing in the opposite direction. Her heart felt like it stopped for at least a minute when it dawned on her that that said guy was in fact Chris. She gulped.

"Hey, you! What are you doing here?" She feared she had overdone it with the 'surprised' look on her face.

"Where's your phone? I've been trying to ring you!"

She was trying to discreetly turn her phone off behind her back so that she could pretend that the battery had gone.

"Did you enjoy the match?"

"I just asked you a question!" Chris's voice was getting louder, and it wasn't in order to be heard over the music, "Where's Andie?"

"Who?" she replied quickly, with a quiver in her voice. For a moment she thought he had said 'Anthony' until she realised what he had actually said. "Oh, Andie, she's just gone!"

"So why are you still here?" Chris continued with his suspicious line of questioning.

"Me? Well, I wanted an extra dance and the toilet, then I saw what's his name that you play with, and he said you might be joining him, so I thought I'd wait and ring you, but my battery died, but now you're here, so it's fine!" Her ramblings did nothing to remove the inquisitive look on Chris's face.

"So why were you so surprised to see me if you knew I might be coming down, or was it a look of guilt instead?"

She was continuing to glance around the room to see if she could see Antony, the combination of her nerves and alcohol consumption making her very indiscreet.

"I'm talking to you! Who are you looking for?" Chris scowled.

"Looking for? Er, no-one, well actually I was looking for your mate!"

"Why are you looking for him? Do you fancy him or something?" Chris seethed.

Just as Chris was about to erupt, she saw Anthony making his way towards the entrance of the club. He threw her a wink and blew her a kiss before he disappeared out of the door. She smiled, completely forgetting herself and who she was stood in front of.

"Who the fuck are you smiling at?" Chris's temper removed her feelings of relief and made her realise that she wasn't out of the woods just yet.

"No one, I'm just drunk!"

"Yes, a drunken flirt as per! We're going home! Now!"

"Now?" she wasn't bothered about going home, she'd had enough excitement for one day, but she wanted to delay him slightly in case Anthony hadn't moved his car and set off yet.

"Yes, NOW!"

"Can I just go to the toilet first, please?"

"No! Move it now, don't make a show of me, Mel, I mean it!"

"OK, I'm coming!" She didn't want to push things; she knew she was in for it anyway for going out and not telling him in the first place, and now he thinks she's been flirting with his teammates, his treatment towards her would be unbearable.

They walked towards the entrance. Melissa had everything crossed that Anthony had now had more than enough time to get away and that he would now be completely out of sight. Then she remembered the text she had sent and the phone calls she had made. Chris would be checking her phone for sure once they got home, so she needed to find a way to delete the messages and phone calls, but she had no idea how she would manage it, as she would be sat next to him all the way home.

"Where are you parked? My feet are hurting; can you please bring the car to the door instead of me having to walk to it?" she asked, hopeful that this would allow her some time to clear any interaction with Anthony from her phone.

"Are you taking the piss?" She took that as a no and continued to follow him out of the club. The air felt even cooler than it was previously, or maybe that was just because of the company that she now found herself in. She glanced over to where Anthony had parked only to see that he was gone, so she breathed out loudly with a sigh of relief.

"What are you doing? Making stupid noises?" Chris looked at her like she was a leper or something.

"Oh, I just felt a bit sick once the air hit me, so I was just taking a breath."

"Well, you better not be sick in my car, you silly bitch!"

As he marched across the road to where his car was parked, she realised he had parked only two spots away from where Anthony had parked. 'He arrived before Ant went, he must have seen it. He must have!' She took another large breath out, as this time, an actual bout of queasiness churned in her stomach.

He glared at her across the roof of the car as he stood at the driver's door. She clasped her hand on the front passenger door but didn't open it, as he hadn't opened his door. She stared back at him, trying to figure out if he had noticed Anthony's car or not.

"Well, get in then, or are you waiting for someone?" he bellowed.

Melissa didn't even reply; she couldn't, she was so taken aback by his comment, she just quickly got in the car. Chris gave nothing away during the ride home; he was silent; the silent treatment wasn't unusual for him to dish out when he was annoyed with her, and it could sometimes last for days. However, this time she was unsure whether he was keeping silent in order to stop himself from saying something, or if he was plotting something? Why wasn't he demanding to check her phone? She was absolutely convinced that he had seen Anthony's car; she just knew he had in her gut, but she didn't know at what moment he was going to let her know that he had seen it.

CHAPTER 12.

TOO CLOSE FOR COMFORT

Her Sunday morning lie-in was disturbed by the noise of the rain that was bouncing down outside; a typical British summer seemed to now be creeping in. She rolled over, pulling the duvet over her shoulder, and reached for her phone. She stretched further to reach for her 'secret SIM' from the hiding place within a pair of socks at the back of her bedside drawer - that had been the safest place that she could think to keep it when it wasn't in her bra that is.. Just before she changed over the SIM, she climbed out of bed and tiptoed to the window to double-check Chris's car had gone just in case he hadn't already left for his rugby match like she presumed. She carefully peered out of the window, peeking through a gap in the curtains and she was relieved to see that his car was gone. The huge raindrops seemed like they were doing a victory dance on her behalf, jumping up and down on the driveway and her car. She got back in bed and nestled under the warm covers, lifted off the back of her phone and placed it down on top of the covers. Then she removed the battery and switched over her SIM. Chris had been at home most of yesterday evening, as it was a pre-match night, and he was still giving her the cold shoulder from last Saturday (which only reinforced the fact that she was sure that he had seen Anthony's car) so she hadn't managed to speak to Anthony since yesterday morning and she was starting to get withdrawals. She turned her phone back on and 5 messages came through from Anthony. She smiled; she was never disappointed by a lack of messages. Every time she turned on her phone, she was met with message alerts providing her with a warm comforting feeling. The *knowing* that 'he'd been thinking of her as much as she had him'.

FROM ANTHONY - MISS U XX LOVE U XX

FROM ANTHONY - I HATE IT WHEN WE CANT TALK! I'LL MEET U IN MY DREAMS XX

She chuckled at the corniness of that message.

FROM ANTHONY - CHRIS HAS BEEN QUIZZING LOUISA ABOUT WHERE I WAS LAST SATURDAY NIGHT! WHY WOULD HE DO THAT? XX

Her stomach churned a little.

FROM ANTHONY - HE HAS GRILLED HER SO MUCH SHE'S BEEN REALLY QUESTIONING ME. HE SAID HE SAW MY CAR IN TOWN? XX

"Oh fuck! I knew it!" She said as she slammed her hands on her head. She moved them away so that she could read the last message, which she noticed was only sent 15 minutes ago. Her palms began to sweat; she knew that he had seen Anthony's car, (she hadn't shared that worry with Anthony though, as she didn't see the point in him getting overwhelmed with anxiety in the same way she was, just in case she was wrong.)

FROM ANTHONY – STUART'S JUST WALKED IN THE DOOR, CHRIS MATCH IS OFF COZ OF THE RAIN. HE'LL BE HOME SOON. I

HOPE U GET THIS? BE CAREFUL I THINK HE KNOWS XXXX

Chris knew, he ...knew, and this time she absolutely knew that he knew, and he was on his way home, probably gunning for her. Her hands were shaking as she frantically tried to swap her 'Anthony' SIM from her phone back to standard SIM. The house phone started ringing, but she didn't answer, she couldn't, she needed to put her phone back together. Then it started ringing again, this time she thought it was best that she answered it as he would only keep ringing and her not answering would infuriate him more. "Hello?" Her voice was shaking. "Melissa, what is going on, where's your mobile?" Chris fumed down the phone. "Something is going on with you, your phone is never on, you're not answering the house phone, what the FUCK is going on? I know you; you're hiding something, you've changed!"

Even though she wasn't in love with Chris anymore and it wasn't like she wanted to salvage their relationship at all, she was scared of him and what he might do. She knew for certain he would get payback somehow and that 'somehow' scared her terribly.

"I, I, I've just got out of the shower, for God's sake, that's why I've not answered the house phone. My battery has gone on my mobile and I have told you a million times I can't have my phone at work anymore; they have gone really strict."

"Really?"

"Yes!"

"REALLY!"

"Yes, Chris, what's wrong with you? Stop shouting!"

"Well, why are you stuttering? When you stutter it's usually because your lying!"

The phone went dead, "Oh fuck!" her chest rose as she inhaled deeply. She could hear a car screeching onto the drive, splashing through the large puddles. She looked down at her other SIM card on the bed. Her heart started racing fast - it was pounding so hard; it was as if it were about to bound out of her chest. Her hands were trembling, so she was barely able to remove the back of the phone. The car door slammed. She swiped frantically at the back of the phone and finally, the back flew off, tumbling across the floor. She flicked up the battery pack and slid the SIM card out with ease as it stuck to the clamminess of her fingertips. The front door slammed shut. 'Shit!' Scrambling to pick the back of the phone up off the floor, one SIM card pinged on to the bed as she picked up her other SIM card. Her trembling hands were not helping at all. She tried to replace her SIM card, then she realised that she couldn't transfer it in time. 'When he sees my phone stripped apart, he will start questioning, then he'll start searching, and he won't stop!' Her head started spinning, her palms started sweating and she could feel herself hyperventilating.

"Melissa!" The door slammed.

It suddenly dawned on her that she had said she had just gotten out of the shower, yet she was still stood there, fully clothed, wearing the same pyjamas that she had on yesterday evening.

She quickly scooped up the back of the phone and battery off the bed, along with the 'Anthony' SIM card and raced to the bathroom.

"I'll be down in a minute, I just need the toilet!" she yelled, as she dashed across the landing to the bathroom.

She ran in and slammed the door without thinking, 'Shit! Shit! Shit!'

She nearly ripped her pyjamas off, before grabbing a towel from the rail to wrap around her.

Melissa glanced on to the sink unit where her phone lay in two pieces along with her SIM card of shame.

She picked up the SIM, and without a second thought, she threw it down the toilet, stood watching as she flushed it away, feeling slightly disloyal to Anthony in the process. She felt pained as she watched their 'love letters' disappear.

The floor started vibrating as he started running up the stairs, the toilet stopped flushing and the SIM had disappeared. She nearly collapsed with relief and let out a huge breath.

BANG, BANG, BANG!

"What are you doing?" a thunderous voice bellowed from the other side of the door.

"For goodness sake, Chris, I've been on the toilet, I told you I needed the toilet," she shouted. As she pretended to wash her hands, she threw the water onto the front of her hair and wrapped a towel around her head.

"Well, get out here!" Chris proceeded in banging on the door, extremely hard and very loud, "I'll kick the fucking thing down in a minute! Get out here now!"

"Fuck's sake, Chris, what's your problem? Can I not even have a wee anymore?" She opened the door before he could bang it down, glaring at him to try and disguise her nervousness.

"You what? Who do you think you're talking to?' He got right in her face, pressing his head up against hers with just enough force and pressure to make her feel intimidated.

She could tell by the look on his face he was not impressed.

"You're up to something and I want to know what it is! Why is your phone off? I thought you said you had to have it off at work?'

'I do!'

'Well, it's a Sunday and your phone has just been off and you're at home, so what's going on?'

"Er, my battery went, I told you!" Her heart started pounding again - just what did he know?

"Yes, you did tell me that and I don't believe you!" He grabbed her face forcefully, "Don't lie to me!" he demanded through gritted teeth.

'What if his teammate saw me with Anthony? What if he's told him on the way to training? Oh God!' her questions whizzed around her head

"I'm not lying to you; I haven't even said anything."

"Exactly!" he glanced down at the phone that she was clasping in her trembling hands. "What are you doing with that, why is it in pieces?"

"Er, I, er…" 'Think! Say something,' she was urging herself to speak up and say something, anything.

Chris snatched the pieces of her phone out of her hands and stormed into the bedroom. Her 'pre-Anthony' SIM was in clear view on the bed - at least she hoped it was her pre-Anthony SIM; for a split second she began to wonder whether in the sheer panic of it all, that she had flushed the wrong one.

He picked it up with an arrogant 'I'm going to catch you out' look on his face.

By this point, Melissa had begun trying to explain that she had taken the SIM out to clean it then dozed off, but her voice was zoned out by Chris as he demanded that she handed over her phone, and he pieced it back together. He switched on the phone, staring right at her, and she gulped as she questioned again whether she had flushed away the wrong SIM. The phone beeped to signaling it was switching on. She wondered, was he about to open up the sea of texts between her and Anthony? Was every aspect of their confessions of love and steamy lust-fuelled trysts about to be exposed?

She stood completely still for what felt like forever, just trying to read his face for any reactions. The anticipation built; Chris stood scouring call lists and messages but to no avail. Her whole body relaxed as she realised that it was the correct SIM that she had discarded.

Clearly frustrated by his lack of evidence, Chris erupted, "I know you're up to something!" He barged past Melissa and left the room. She collapsed on the bed, sinking into it, running her hands over her face and back down again with sheer relief. That emotional was quickly struck by a pang of guilt and made her extremely uneasy. She was being the type of person she despised. She didn't love Chris, she knew that. 'You just need to end it,' she thought, 'you can't just carry on having an affair' especially one that was becoming more and more serious each week. 'What am I doing?'

After the close call with the SIM card this morning, Melissa was absolutely dreading the monthly Sunday dinner ritual façade at Chris's parents. She knew that Chris would be scrutinising her every move. He obviously didn't have anything solid, otherwise he would have blown by now, but he certainly had his suspicions and that he wouldn't stop now until he got his evidence. She couldn't stomach the thought of sitting around the table acting all innocent and lying to so many people, no matter how much or how little she liked them, she simply couldn't stand this side of her relationship with Anthony. Although in so many ways she felt like she was coming back to life and becoming more like her old self every day, she actually also felt more and more removed from her old self as she never thought she would ever have an affair. When it was just her and Anthony, she found it so much easier to ignore the fact that her new love was, in fact, somebody else's boyfriend. She could ignore the fact that her new movie-like love was actually built on a foundation of lies and she also convinced herself that the reason she hadn't told Chris yet that she didn't want to be with him anymore was because the timing wasn't right. Mainly as she didn't have enough money saved or anywhere to go. 'Where would I go?'

The wave of questions came in her head, one after another. Not giving herself chance to answer

194

any of them before she stopped at 'why is Anthony still with Louisa?' He didn't have a mortgage with her, no children, they weren't married, he could just stay at home? He'd briefly touched on his home life in the past but it wasn't like he doesn't have options. If things are 'bad' with Louisa, what exactly was stopping him?' He could end things today with very little repercussions, so why didn't he? She started to wonder if her white knight was quite as white as he made out? Was he simply turning her into one of 'those women' and having his cake and eating it?

After the mass questioning in her head, she knew in order to get answers to them all, it was time to have a serious conversation with Anthony. She couldn't be afraid of rocking the boat anymore; it was time to ask the question that is scary enough to ask in any relationship - where are we going with this? She wasn't even sure why she was so scared about asking him that question, considering he had professed his love to her before their relationship had even begun and had continued to do so several times thereafter. But something had begun to niggle at her when she realised that this affair had now spanned over 8 weeks, and not once had he mentioned or hinted at the fact that he was near to ending things with Louisa. She also decided that she needed a trip to the bank on Monday to check the balance of her secret account and try and calculate the minimum amount she needed in order to escape. "As soon as I hit that amount, I'm done! I can and I will go!" She smiled after making the declaration to herself in the mirror. She wanted to ensure she had solid plans so that when she had 'the' conversation with Anthony, he couldn't turn things around on her and question why she was still with Chris. She wanted straight answers from him, and she didn't want him charming his way out of the conversation. (Something that deep down she knew he was more than capable of!) Whenever she had touched on the subject previously, she had been quickly distracted with him romancing her and overwhelming her with compliments. Realisation had hit in and as nice a world as that it was to live in, but it wasn't a real one she thought. She had to find out what his intentions were.

Trying to convince herself she was doing the right thing 'rocking the boat' she then told herself: "I won't be happy living with these snatched moments of happiness all the time and then all the hours of dread and worry that comes with it." A trending doubt of guilt washed over her.

"Right, I'm back. Are you ready or what?" Her thought-sparring session had been interrupted by an extremely moody Chris bellowing upstairs.

"Yes, I'm ready.... two minutes and I'll be down!"

"Make sure you look nice!" he demanded.

"I do!" she replied, whilst rolling her eyes at the cheek of both his demanding tone and the context of his demands.

"Yeah, well, I'll decide that!" he scathed.

Melissa didn't even bother responding to such a rude, obnoxious and controlling statement. Instead of feeling beaten down by such comments. Even after this morning, and the fear she felt, his attitude and controlling ways had stirred up a fire in her belly again and she made a promise to herself that she wasn't going to let him get to her today. She looked lovely; she was wearing a pair of light blue denim jeans with a slight flare, a pink cotton, fitted DKNY top and some pink stiletto heels. it was the perfect look for a chilled Sunday dinner with the in-laws. As she reached the bottom of the stairs, Chris scowled at her, blatantly looking her up and down judging her whole attire. Ironically, he was merely wearing a tracksuit. Then he clasped his car keys in his hands before grunting, "You'll do!"

"Thank you!" her reply oozed sarcasm, as did her smile.

He glared at her, unimpressed by her attitude, so she intensified her false smile even further, knowing full well that it would completely wind him up. She had started to learn that the less she cried and bothered about what he said or did to her, then the less he prodded and poked at her. Oddly quite the opposite in fact - he seemed almost sheepish, completely unsure of what to do when she acted confident and aloof to his demanding and controlling behaviour. However, in the sheer panic of this morning, the power of such knowledge had been wiped from her mind. So she made sure that now, she'd keep her weapon at the forefront of her mind at all times, especially this afternoon.

She followed him out the front door. But as quick as her confident pep talk was over, the nerves crept straight back in. 'Can I handle this, a whole afternoon with Chris, his full family and Anthony?' She questioned her strength. "You can do this; you can do this!" she spurred herself on under her breath.

As they took their seats around the dinner table, Melissa found herself facing Anthony as well as being sat right next to Chris. Louisa, Chris and their mum Jackie, and dad Richard, their older brother Stuart and sister Cath were all there too. Jackie and Richard of course sat at each end of the table, taking up their positions as heads of the family. Jackie looked polished from head to toe; she was a very glamourous lady but one who was stuck in a time warp. She'd regularly don exaggerated shoulder pads which made her look like she had just stepped out of the '80s. Richard wasn't a man of many words - much like Chris - but the words he did utter were usually very authoritative, bolshy, sexist and chauvinistic. He wore his shirt open to show off his large gold medallion chain that lay nestled against his hairy chest. Chris idolised his dad. But more recent Melissa felt she was looking at Chris in 25 years' time whenever she saw Richard. And each time since, she wanted to run away from her life as fast as she could. Chris's older brother Stuart on the other hand, looked nothing like Chris or his dad. He had dark hair and soft chocolate brown eyes, as did Cath, who spent most of her time at university in Birmingham.

Melissa glanced around the table, cleverly avoiding any eye contact with anyone, especially Anthony. She suddenly felt uneasy, like a complete fraud. It had been bad enough hiding things from Chris, but she had always justified that to herself by his ongoing horrendous behaviour. But now it was the whole family in front of her and it suddenly dawned on her that Chris wasn't the only one she was betraying. She started to feel pangs of anxiety as her mind raced again. Someone is bound to pick up on a look or the body language between her and Anthony and it suddenly became all too apparent that this was far too close for comfort. This was the first time into the 8-week affair that they had all gathered at the Clancy's for Sunday dinner. She continued to avoid any eye contact with Anthony or anyone else for that matter, which only added to her paranoia. But she couldn't bear to look anyone in the eye, she felt so ashamed of her recent actions. She tried to stick to conversations down at the other end of the table, whilst keeping her eyes mainly focused on her plate of food. Her emotional torture quickly changed as she could feel herself starting to fill with jealousy. As out of the corner of her eye she' caught Louisa affectionately rubbing the back of Anthony's neck and she couldn't bear it – 'they don't look like a couple on the rocks' she thought to herself.

"What do you think, Mel?" She was suddenly jolted from her distracting thoughts back into conversation with Stuart. He had always been lovely to Melissa, as had Cath, their older sister. They took after their mum's side of the family, whereas Chris and Louisa had their dad's arrogant Clancy genes running through them like a stick of rock. All three acted like pack leaders, like they were superior to the others, and the others just let them.

"Erm, sorry Stuart, I didn't catch that, what were you saying?" She felt embarrassed, feeling like she had been caught out with her mind elsewhere. She could feel Anthony's eyes burning holes into her; she knew he wanted her to look at him, but she just couldn't. She was engaged in the conversation with Stuart and Jackie when she felt a foot slowly rubbing up the outside of her calf. She immediately lost her train of thought again; she was furious, what was Anthony doing? She could see Stuart and Jackie patiently waiting for her to expand on what she was saying, "I'm so sorry, I've forgotten what I was saying now, sorry, I've gone a bit dizzy." Stuart chuckled playfully, "You're always a bit dizzy!"

She put her hand on her forehead and under the table she tried to discreetly shove Anthony's foot away.

"Oh sorry, Zippy – I think I was just playing footsie with you then; I thought it was Louisa's leg!" She couldn't believe what was coming out of Anthony's mouth or his actions – was he getting off on this? Everyone laughed, bar Chris, and she couldn't help but instinctively throw him a dirty look. She was so upset with him, like this situation wasn't bad enough!

"Oh, I didn't even notice, don't worry – I really don't feel well – I'm sorry Jackie, I think I need to lie down." She wasn't lying - her head started spinning and she felt like she couldn't catch her breath, her anxiety levels were increasing by the second and she had to get out of there - immediately!

"Are you ok?" Chris asked her, with what seemed like real affection. He reassuringly placed his hand on her knee, and she instantly felt worse, bemused by his rare showing of affection, although he was particularly good at doing that for show! She felt her eyes welling up. "I will be, I just, please, I need to lie down."

Chris accompanied her upstairs onto the bed in his old room. He unnervingly kissed her forehead and left the room, seeming genuinely concerned as he shut the door behind him. She rarely saw it these days but that was a glimmer of Chris and the nature he had when they had first got together. Her tears poured out uncontrollably down her face, she felt like such a horrible person, she barely recognised herself anymore. Just when she thought she was finding herself again, the entirety of the whole situation was so real and everyone it would affect had been right there, sat around the dining table, smiling at her and offering such warm hospitality. She couldn't believe the person she had become. Even in Cyprus she hadn't felt this bad, as she hadn't consciously made that decision, but for this situation there was no excuse - she felt selfish and as if she was displaying all of the traits that she despised in Chris.

She wasn't just upset with herself, she felt so disappointed and angry with Anthony. She couldn't understand what he was trying to achieve. She began to feel like a plaything in some sort of sick joke. Was that all it was to him, a joke? Was he just pushing the boundaries to see what he could get away with? She felt sick and totally exhausted; she had endured so many years of tiresome mind games with Chris, she didn't have the energy to try and figure out what was going on in Anthony's head now as well. She then switched to an overwhelming fury towards Chris 'Why is he being nice to me anyway? Pretending to care, I bet, just for show like normal. If he would have just been a nice normal boyfriend anyway, then none of this would have ever happened!' She hated it when he was nice these days - it spooked her more than when he was vile and tormentative because it made her feel like the bad one and guilty for betraying him despite all he had done. "I can't do this anymore, I can't, I don't feel well, I don't feel well!" she sobbed as she mumbled into the pillow in despair.

She heard the floorboards on the landing creak; someone was heading towards the bedroom and so she leaned further into the pillow, facing the wall in an attempt to hide her face and fake sleep. She couldn't deal with anyone's sympathy, asking how she was; if only they knew, she knew they wouldn't care at all then. The door handle went down, so she lay as still as she could, her eyes closed, and her face was down in the pillow that was sodden from all her tears. She felt someone sit on the bed and she knew immediately who it was as she inhaled his intoxicating aftershave and she smiled instinctively despite feeling so cross at him.

"Hey, Liss, are you ok?" Anthony uttered softly as he stroked her arm with his thumb "I know you're not asleep sexy, come on, what's up?" That really riled her as she shot up from the pillow filled with a hundred different emotions. "What's up, Anthony? What the fuck's up?! Are you really asking me that question? Are you as sick in the head as him? Do me a favour and go away!!"

"Go away, Liss? Don't be like that! I wanted to check you were, ok?" he said as he grabbed both her arms and looked into her eyes passionately. "I love you; you know that don't be like this," he leant towards her face. "No, I don't know that Anthony, I don't know anything anymore. This isn't right - we can't do this anymore, we just can't - I can't." Anthony gently kissed her cheek, and removing his hands from her arms, he lifted her chin, wiped away her tears and firmly placed his hands on her cheeks. "Melissa, I love you, and you love you me, so how can that be wrong? We'll sort it, ok?" She didn't want to; her head was screaming for her to push him off, but she looked longingly into his beautiful blue eyes and as he began to passionately kiss her she couldn't help but kiss him back. She had lost her mind to him again and had completely zoned out of where she was. Within moments, the sound of laughter echoed up the stairs and remembering exactly where she was, she pushed Anthony away. "Are you crazy? Some kind of adrenaline junkie or something? Louisa, *YOUR* Louisa and the whole bloody family are downstairs! Have you seriously lost the plot, because I have, I MUST have," she rambled frantically with mixed emotions racing through her and the tears again streaming down her cheeks.

"Of course, it's not easy, but it's their own fault, Liss. We're not the ones who have done wrong if they would have treated us right in the first place." "Anthony," Melissa jumped in, "just because they can be arse holes, it doesn't make what we are doing ok you know – what we are doing is bad, really bad – and I can't," she paused unable to look at him, "I can't do it anymore."

"Don't say that Liss, please!"

"I can't, Ant. I'm going to finish it with Chris tonight and I'm not going to see you again until you finish with Louisa."

"Ok, I will."

"I'm not demanding it, Anthony, you do whatever you want to do; I'm not leaving Chris for you, I'm leaving him for my own sanity; I should have done it years ago, I just didn't have the courage until now." The tears had stopped, and she found strength in her own words, knowing that something had clicked, and it was now or never. "I mean it, Anthony though, these aren't just empty words, I've spouted them out enough to last me a lifetime. Unless we are both single, this needs to end, here and now! I despise people who do this type of thing and I'm just starting to find a love for myself again, but I can't really do that if I'm ashamed of myself at the same time. You do understand, don't you?"

"Yes, I do, it will all be ok, I will tell Louisa when we have found somewhere to live. Honestly, it will all be ok, I'll look after you," he embraced her, but she found herself a little dumbfounded by his reaction. 'Live?' She didn't expect that at all; they had only been seeing each other for a couple of months and whilst they were both with other people, it most certainly wasn't the foundation to decide to set up home together – 'live?' she couldn't believe what she had heard.

This was all getting so out of control, the term out of the frying pan and into the fire rang aloud in her head. After they pulled out of the embrace, she studied his face; he was actually serious, he really wanted them to move in together. She didn't know where to start to try and put things right.

The merry-go-round in her mind halted, as she heard someone running upstairs. Anthony moved to the other end of the bed quickly, saying, "Pretend to be asleep!" He let go of her hand and gestured for her to lie down quickly.

The bedroom door opened; it was Louisa. "What are you doing, Ant?"

"Shhh! She's asleep. I went to the toilet and thought I would check on Zippy. I've done my first aid at work now, haven't I?"

Louisa cackled, "You are such a dick! That doesn't make you a nurse you know, leave her alone."

He got off the bed and left the room and they closed the door behind them. Melissa turned onto her back, gazing up at the dated woodchip ceiling, as she replayed how coolly Anthony just handled that, no quiver in his voice, no hesitation in his words, he seemed to be always one step ahead, it was like it came naturally to him, like he had done it before. He was completely unfazed, and in that moment, for the first time since his first few texts, she began to question his true intentions and whether she could trust him. Then the words 'when we find somewhere to live' rang aloud in her ears. Was she just moving from one bad situation straight into another? As much as she had developed overwhelming feelings for Anthony and she was completely certain now that she did love him, the thought of just shacking up with him straight away made her feel uneasy; it was absurd that he would even want too as well. This cloak and dagger relationship was far from a solid basis to move in together and her white knight once again seemed to be showing chinks in his armour. Suddenly, she knew the road ahead, even with Anthony, was going to be far from a smooth one.

CHAPTER 13.

I DON'T LOVE YOU ANYMORE

When they returned home that evening, Melissa just plonked herself onto the couch.

She didn't even bother turning on any of the lamps. Chris went straight into the kitchen, "I'll get you a glass of water and you better go straight to bed, or you might not be up for work tomorrow." The noise from the tap running stopped and he entered the living room, holding out the glass of water towards her.

"I don't love you anymore, Chris. I haven't for a long time now so please don't tell me that I do, because I don't, ok? I don't love you; I don't love you anymore!"

She had finally found the strength and the courage to utter the words that had sat on the tip of her tongue for so long. She had always choked previously when she had tried to say them but today, they just kept coming out. She had told him; she had done it and she was completely and utterly thrown by his reaction. All the bravado and macho exterior had melted away and uncovered a lost little boy. As he slumped against the couch and immediately started sobbing what seemed like a thousand tears, Melissa found herself lost as to how to react. She had an overwhelming urge to reach out and hold him, he was so sad, and her instinct was to try and make him feel better. She was battling with herself in her mind; she didn't want to undo what it had taken her so long to do, but it went against her nature to sit back coldly and see someone hurting, even if that person had hurt her too many times to count. Eventually, her softer side gave in, and she sat on the oak laminate floor next to him, hesitantly placing her arm around his shoulders. "Chris don't be upset, you know as well as I do it's not right between us – this isn't a relationship. It's just, it's like a habit, a toxic habit that we don't know how to give up – we'll be happier apart."

"NO!" he glanced upwards at her face as he put his hands on either cheek firmly looking right in her eyes, "I know I've made mistakes; I know I have, but we can make it right, we can!"

"No, we can't, Chris, it's too late, it's far too late—I don't…"

"Stop it! Don't say it again!" He covered his ears like a child and started rocking. "Please, Mel – I love you, I do, just give me one more chance, please, things will be different, I promise, please, I promise," his breakdown was becoming more and more intense. The conversation that followed combed through their relationship from start to finish and it was exhausting.

She remained next to him on the floor, cradling his head as he wept into her chest. She had feelings towards him, new feelings, but they weren't love or of the romantic kind, they were feelings of pity. She hadn't expected it to be this way, she had braced herself for a physical battle with him, the one she had always been so frightened of facing, but instead she watched him crumble before her very eyes. It took her totally by surprise and now she feared that without saying 'yes' or in any way agreeing to anything, her actions had somehow led Chris to believe there was some hope for them and that they were to give it another try. As he sobbed, she had never felt guiltier over her feelings for Anthony. Staring into space she didn't know what move she should make next. Was she in part to blame, because she let Chris walk all over her so of course he was going to want his own way all the time? Why wouldn't he take advantage of the fact that if he said jump, she would always reply how high? He was right; she hadn't ever properly said how she was feeling, she might have tried a few times, but she never seemed to make him listen, not like today, not like now – what if the penny had dropped, what if he could change, if he could be how he was when they first started out, back when she was happy, before that awful night that took her away? They did have a house together, a life together – well, in some form. She felt confused and her lack of support and other options in life didn't really help her at present. It was 10:45 pm. Melissa felt completely drained from raw emotion that had been pushing through her from the moment she took a seat at that table. It was 7.07 pm when she had uttered the words 'I don't love you anymore'. It seemed like only 5 minutes earlier, yet at the same time, it felt like she had been sat there for weeks almost. She looked to see if Chris had fallen asleep, but he hadn't, he was just staring with a completely blank expression; he looked broken, and it crushed her to think she was responsible for doing that to someone.

"Chris let's go to bed. I'm shattered and you look really tired too." He didn't agree or disagree, he just started to move. They got up almost in slow motion using the couch and each other to lift their weary bodies from the floor. Her legs felt heavy as she dragged each one slowly upstairs. The stresses and strains of not just the last couple of hours but the last couple of years seemed to be having a physical impact on Melissa and she couldn't wait to rest her war-torn body. She followed behind Chris, watching as he too seemed to be suffering from the same problem; he looked like he was carrying a heavy load. She had seen flickers of it before with him, but he had never opened up enough for her to get to the root of any issues he may have had. Any issues that she wondered may be behind the way he treated her. She had always tried to find out what they may be as she wanted to help him, but he would shut down immediately and snap back at her if she ever dared to hint that something was troubling him. They lay down on the bed, silent, still and still very much separate from each other. Melissa felt comfier and lighter as she lay there; she was proud she had found the strength inside to take action and whatever ended up coming of it now could only be for the better. The curtains were wide open as neither of them could be bothered to draw them. The wind was picking up and Melissa watched the tree in front the window dancing wildly to and fro, catching glimpses of the stars between the moving branches. She knew Chris was awake also, but she didn't know what to say; she almost felt like she didn't know him; after all, she had never seen like this before.

She watched him leave for work the next morning, his hopeful smile and his constant turning back to wave to her at the upstairs window left her feeling nauseous. She was angered by his arrogance that her words meant nothing, but also sad that she now could finally see just how weak he was.

She felt like she had aged at least two years overnight, and until she was completely free of his clutches, she decided that she had to put her and Anthony completely on hold. She just couldn't take it anymore; her nerves were completely shot. She could feel her sadness mounting as she picked up the phone, her hands trembled, and she blinked away the tears that she knew would soon turn into a river-like stream. She began typing to Anthony. Her heart was heavy, as was her mind. What she was about to do was definitely not coming from the heart. Her head battled away with her heart right up until the moment she pressed send - and she hadn't even reached the hard part yet.

TO ANTHONY - R U WITH LOUISA? I CAN'T SEEM TO GET THROUGH TO HER ON HER PHONE.

Of course, she didn't really want Louisa, it was their code sentence only to be used in emergencies.

Within less than a minute her phone rang, so she took a deep breath, bracing herself for a conversation she knew wouldn't be easy, nor did she even really want to have it, she just knew that unless something changed - right now - that something terrible would end up happening. Seeing Chris so broken made her even more fearful about what he would do to Anthony if he were to find out about their affair; no matter how much he had annoyed her yesterday, she just couldn't risk him ending up hurt, or worse, still losing him for good. If Chris thought he had lost everything already anyway, who knew how dark his dark side could turn!

She had decided to do it before work, firstly so she didn't spend the day talking herself out of it, and secondly so that could fall into the supportive arms of Colette and Liz. She knew that they would help her stay strong and stick to whatever decision she decided to make, no matter what they thought; throughout all of this, they had never once judged her and constantly supported her.

She took another deep breath and answered the phone.

"Hello!"

"Hello beautiful, what's up? Is everything ok?"

"Not really Ant, no," her voice started to quiver, "the thing is" she took a pause, a long pause and then had the conversation she would have done anything not to have.

She was right to think that she would have needed the girls in such circumstances, as she felt truly devastated inside. (It was a first for her to do something like this at a time when she knew that before long, she would soon be surrounded by lots of people, instead of hiding away and dealing with her upset and emotions all alone).

It had probably been the hardest conversation she had ever had, much, much harder than telling Chris that she no longer loved him, even harder than opening an old wound and telling Anthony about what had happened in Cyprus. Hearing Anthony beg for her to reconsider, telling her that he didn't care about the consequences, that he didn't even want one day without her, was just heart-wrenching. He sobbed and sobbed, as did she, but underneath all the feelings of hurt and the piles of tissues she had gone through, she knew that for her own sanity she was doing the right thing. Even though she had told Chris that she didn't love him anymore, Anthony had barely offered any such reciprocal act, and despite his protests, he could only offer a half murmur that he would tell Louisa when the time was right. When she raised the issue with him, his defence was that if he did it now it would look completely suspicious, so he was therefore holding off for their own good as much as he hated being with her for even a moment longer. One half of her believed him and understood his logic completely, but the other half of her felt like she was being played - but the whole of her loved him, and finally she had told him that. In fact, that was how she ended the emotional phone call. "I love you, Anthony, I really do, but I just can't do this anymore", and with that, she put the phone down and began Operation Cold Turkey.

She continued to cry all the way to work, re-applying her makeup in the car park before heading into the office. Her old ritual of leaving the radio off, so as not to invoke any further emotion returned, today though, this old faithful coping mechanism couldn't help her hide away her emotions. The old feminist inside her reared its head again and she felt a little angry at herself for being so emotionally ruled by another man that she wasn't even truly sure was genuine.

As soon as she set foot in the office, Colette piped up, "Oh honey, what on Earth is the matter?". There was no 'Morning sweetie pie!' this morning as she peered over her computer, as she could immediately see-through Melissa's attempt at hiding her emotions behind the mask of makeup.

Melissa's bottom lip trembled as soon as the questioned was asked and Colette gave Liz 'the eyes' as she spun around on her office chair to see why Col had asked the question in the first place.

"Ah, your here Mel, great! Me and Col have been waiting for you; we need a quick meeting about this marketing campaign as we need to tweak a few things before it begins on Thursday." Always good in a crisis, Liz had already spun Melissa around before anyone else noticed her face and Colette jumped up, dashing over to the meeting book, as she shouted out after them, "Yes, you two go ahead, I'll just sign us out!"

They made their way down the corridor to meeting room 3 - the one without any interior windows, so she could break down away from any prying eyes, something they had all needed at least once or twice whilst working here.

They sat down, just as Colette rushed through the door like a tornado of concern, slamming the door swiftly behind her and rushing straight over to Melissa. They said nothing, they just put their arms around her, let her tears fall and waited patiently for the words to follow. She explained everything that had happened, everything that finally led her to telling Chris she didn't love him and everything that led her to finally telling Anthony that she did love him, but yet break it off at the same time. Liz and Colette praised her for having such a strong moral compass, then they said very little else other than they were there for her.

TWO WEEKS LATER

Another day, another 5 missed calls and 4 text messages begging her to reconsider. She had gone cold turkey and the withdrawals that she was suffering made her realise that Anthony had become a habit that was more dangerous than cocaine. Her need and want to speak to him felt more like an addiction. She tried everything she could to distract her mind from him, but she knew if she spoke to him, she would crumble. Despite still being mad with him, she was missing him like mad. The past two weeks had been a nightmare; she had cherished every minute of going to work and being surrounded by the girls, their non-important problems and gulping one too many Mocha Choca Lattés to make up for her lack of sleep, as her mind was too busy talking herself out of picking up the phone to Ant and just starting things up again. She knew that despite her ending things firmly stating that they wouldn't and couldn't be together until they were both single and the fact that he still hadn't ended things with Louisa, whenever she felt herself feeling sad, she felt herself weaken and each day she got nearer and nearer to picking up the phone. She had to make herself feel angry with him every day to refuel her determination and stick to her word and her morals.

She had felt completely suffocated by Chris's new-found kindness and appreciation of her; knowing from experience that it would be short-lived, she was willing it to be over sooner rather than later. He was spending most of his evenings at home as he tried to show her that he could be the dutiful boyfriend after all. She wished she had never said that they never talk or have anything to talk about as he painfully tried to strike up conversations that would very quickly fall flat on their face. He showered her with designer gifts that she didn't want. When she insisted that he returned them, he would beg her to keep them, saying that she deserved them even if they weren't together, after all he had put her through. Even though she had reiterated more than once that she didn't love him anymore, her protests were falling on deaf ears, as Chris was adamant that he could make it right between them - hence the over-the-top gifts and suffocating behaviour.

CHAPTER 14.

831

Melissa slammed down her glass on her dressing table. Having just downed a glass of rosé wine, she grimaced slightly as she wiped off the trickle of wine that had escaped the corner of her mouth. There was absolutely no way that she could endure tonight without being totally pissed. Tonight, was Stuart's (Chris and Louisa's brother) birthday and the whole group was going out for it - including Anthony, of course. Chris had begged her to go and keep up appearances and for some reason, she didn't have the heart to say no. Melissa had always liked Stuart anyway, and she would have felt bad not going out for his birthday. She applied her lip gloss liberally; it was red, and bold and reflected exactly how she was feeling at this present moment. She cheekily pouted to herself in the mirror and then for a second, she paused and took a deep breath. She was getting ready as if she was heading for a great night out, but realistically the likelihood of that happening would be fairly slim odds. She had Chris desperately trying to win back her emotions, which she knew were long gone, but strangely, she thought she was being kinder by letting him try at least. Knowing that the man who really held her heart would be there made her smile; she couldn't wait to see him, despite her desperately trying to do the right thing and continue breaking things off until they were both officially single. Her smile was closely followed by a sigh when of course it dawned on her that he wouldn't be alone but on the arm of Louisa. This made her feel both angry and sad all in one. All this centre stage in front of all their friends - throw in the standard weekend binge drink, tonight was surely a recipe for disaster. She looked into the mirror; "I'm ready," she shouted down to Chris, indicating for him to phone a taxi. "Well, ready as I'll ever be," she mumbled, raising her eyebrows to herself in the mirror. She checked her bag, "cigarettes, hip flask, lip gloss, powder, money, phone and eyeliner - check!"

She knew once she'd had a couple of drinks that Chris would begin his usual routine of 'you're not having any more', so she had taken a leaf out of Colette's book and bought herself a hip flask, filled it with vodka and created a false bottom in her red leather bag to hide it, so that it wouldn't get taken off her by the bouncers - or Chris, for that matter!

There had been so many lovely days this summer, in between the typical British summer rainy days, that her skin was nicely bronzed, her new diet of love, anxiety, cigarettes, alcohol, and the increase in exercise -aka wild sex- had caused Melissa to lose almost a stone, and although it wasn't through the best lifestyle choices, she looked better than she had in years. She spun from side to side, checking to make sure that both her and her outfit looked the part. She no longer despised looking in the mirror and again, just like her last few nights out, she was pleasantly surprised by what she saw. She had quite a poignant moment when she looked in the mirror and she realised the girl staring back at her was quite beautiful in fact and the girl she was looking at was herself. Since Cyprus, she had always hated her boobs for being too big, her eyes for being too blue and her smile for being too nice - all the things those reps had complimented her on before that fateful night. Tonight though, when she looked in the mirror, she didn't associate those things with that incident; she no longer blamed her body, her face, herself for what happened, something had changed. Maybe it was in light of recent events? Maybe it was since she had told Anthony? She wasn't exactly sure, but she now realised that yes, she had been young and naive, yes, she had been too trusting of people she didn't really know, but she shouldn't have to hide herself away shamefully and apologise for her perceived attractiveness for the rest of her life; she shouldn't and wouldn't let them win.

'They may have taken my dignity away from me that night, but I refuse to let them take all of my happiness out of the rest of my life!' She determinedly stared straight into her own eyes. The combination of the realisation of her own breakthrough and her little pre-party prep talk, made her feel even further empowered - something that was noticeably increasing in her, week on week.

"What are you doing, Melly? For God's sake, the taxi's here!" Chris imploded impatiently, yelling upstairs. The first little slip in his new Mr Nice Guy routine.

"Right, right - I'm coming!" She hid the wine and glass in the wardrobe before heading downstairs.

Chris's eyes enlarged as soon as he clapped eyes on Melissa. She knew instantly that he thought she looked beautiful, but even when he was trying his hardest to be nice to her, he just couldn't bring himself to say it. Then just like the flick of a switch, the old Chris reappeared.

"Who are you getting dressed up for?" he sniped.

"Me!" she replied boldly, without even looking at him, as she confidently started to put on her leather jacket.

"What? As if!" he quipped smugly, "Since when did you care about how you look?" He was unable to hide his irritation of her new-found confidence, despite him trying to conceal this for the last two weeks. She flashed a look at him; she could tell that he was biting his tongue, his face was filled with anguish as he tried to hold back from blurting out some horrible put-down.

Melissa turned away and sighed, "The taxi's here, remember, are you coming or not?" as she started to make her way out of the front door. Chris reached out and grabbed her arm aggressively with an aura of desperation. "Ow! Chris, what you doing? Get off me!"

"You do look alright, you know, you do, you know, pretty!" She was puzzled; she studied his face, it seemed like his eyes were searching for some form of gratitude from her, as if he had made some big gesture. It was as if the more confident Melissa became, the more pathetic he seemed.

"OK, well, thanks, can you let go of my arm now, because you're hurting me?" she said, nodding her head and flicking her eyes down towards her arm until he let go.

He wasn't used to Melissa behaving this way; she had finally found her strength and that took away his power over her. Something switched in his face and his whole demeanour, and she knew that he was finally realising that she had slipped away from his clutches and his visible uneasiness increased. Although he had a funny way of showing it, he did genuinely love her. Now that she had been enlightened by that fact, she had realized he wanted to dim her light for all these years in order that no one else would see her shine and fall for her too. He was in unknown territory, unaware of why Melissa was changing, and he felt completely out of control. 'I'm being nice to her, why is she giving me the brush off? She wants to impress someone else; she is up to something. She's changed, she's like the old Melissa. Who does she think she is? She's not making a fool out of me again!' It was like she could hear the thoughts spilling out of his head. His face became even more visibly angry, and she noticed his fist clenched up into his sweaty palms. "You've got too much makeup on - I think you should take it off!" he demanded.

"What? Have you lost it? There is no way! I won't!" Melissa protested. *The memory of the very first time he ever told her to remove her makeup flashed across her mind vividly, and she could still feel how painfully embarrassing it was. It had happened before they lived together, as she walked down the stairs at his mum's house, (in front of all their friends, including Anthony) as she got to the bottom of the stairs, he burst out laughing and told her that she looked like a clown. He ridiculed her that much that she simply turned around, went back upstairs and took it all off. Like pretty much every other occasion, none of their friends said anything in her defence, despite their obvious discomfort with the situation.*

Her disobedience infuriated Chris and he grabbed her arm again, only he squeezed even harder this time and looked straight into her eyes, "TAKE IT OFF!" his voice was raised now, and his words were strained through gritted teeth.

BEEP, BEEP! The beeps from the taxi driver indicated that it wasn't just Chris who was losing his patience.

"Chris, get your hands off me! I'm not letting you tell me what to do anymore!" He squeezed her arm even tighter as her defiance furthered his frustration. "OW! Let go!" Her arm was burning from his tight grip.

"Fine then!" he exclaimed as he let go of her arm. She felt relieved, victorious almost, that she had stood up to him. Suddenly, Chris forcefully thrust the palm of his hand onto her chin and with his full hand wrapped around the lower part of her face, he squeezed her cheeks tightly, shoving her against the wall, banging the back of her head in the process. He looked completely crazed, and Melissa's body started visibly trembling - he had never been physically violent before- was this where it was going to start? He grabbed her hair with his other hand and dragged her across the living room until they were standing in front of the mirror. He pulled her head back by her hair, she winced with pain and cried out as she looked at what was playing out in the reflection. With his cheek pressed up against hers and the grip on her hair tighter than ever, he moved his hand up from her chin and began to vigorously smudge her makeup all around her face. Her face felt sore, but she desperately tried to hold in her tears. He whispered in her ear, "You should have taken it off; look at what you've made me do now!" he snarled at her in the mirror, released his grip, shoved her into the mantlepiece and turned to walk away.

It took all her strength not to cry, she was so angry; just who did he think was? They both jumped as there was a knock at the door. Chris looked worried, "Get upstairs!" he said, sharply.

"What?"

"You heard me, get upstairs! You're not coming out; I'm going to say you are ill." He was frantically trying to fire out his orders through gritted teeth so that whoever was on the other side of the door wouldn't hear him.

"Why? Are you ashamed of what an arse hole you are?" her lip was quivering, "You're just a coward, Chris, and people should see what you're really like!" She darted across the living room and frantically reached out her shaky hand to open the front door. Chris was hot on her heels but couldn't make it to the door before she opened it. It was Stuart; he looked extremely disturbed, as he had seen exactly what Chris had done when he walked up the driveway from the taxi.

"The taxi driver is getting pissed off waiting," he said, trying to act normal but he just couldn't hide his concern. "Are you ok, Mel?"

"Yes, I …", she didn't get a chance to finish replying before Chris quickly jumped in. "She's fine, she's just not feeling well so she's not coming." He turned to her with a glare in his eyes. "You get yourself to bed and I'll see you in the morning", he said as he kissed her cheek, making her skin crawl and she looked towards Stuart. He furrowed his eyebrows and gave her a half-smile, in a 'I hope you're okay' kind of manner. Although Stuart was Chris's older brother, he wasn't built like Chris, either physically or mentally. In all her years of knowing him, she had never known him to have any sort of conflict with anyone. Chris ushered Stuart off the doorstep and hastily slammed the door behind him. Melissa watched through the window as they walked down the drive towards the taxi, Chris had draped his arm over Stuart's shoulder. She glanced down and caught sight of a framed picture of her and Chris, so she swiped it from the windowsill, sending it flying across the room with an almighty scream. "Argghh!! I hate you! I hate you! I hate you!", she cried, as screaming and sobbing, she fell to her knees on to the fluffy rug and she cradled it, gripping the strands of wool between her fingers. She clung on tightly as streams of tears ran continuously down her chapped face.

After about 20 minutes of hysterical crying, she reached into her handbag, and pulled out her hip flask, downing it in one. She then pulled out her cigarettes and lit up, her hands still trembling. She felt frantic, both in her mind and physically. She wanted, needed, to do something, but she just didn't know what. She marched into the kitchen, still puffing on her cigarette and got a glass out of the cupboard and took a bottle of wine from her secret stash and poured a large red wine. She proceeded to gulp it back as she ran upstairs, unaware of it spilling onto the stair carpet. She placed her glass down on the dresser, opened the bedroom window to dimp out her cigarette, throwing it into the front garden. She pulled a suitcase out from under the bed and started packing wildly, throwing anything and everything that was hers into the case. She didn't care how much money she had saved up, or the fact she had nowhere properly lined up to go to

- she just knew she had to go! She struggled to close the zip and it caused her to break down again. She was sitting on the bed exasperated, with her head hanging in her hands, when her phone bleeped.

FROM ANTHONY - WHERE R U? ME and LOUISA ARE HERE? ARE YOU ON UR WAY? X

He obviously only wanted to know Melissa's whereabouts, but he had to code it so that it didn't look suspicious should Chris see it. It had been the only way for them to communicate again since she had flushed the other SIM card, making it easier for her to blank his messages the last two weeks. Agitated, she began to reply that she wasn't coming, when a wave of insubordination took hold of her. After what had just happened, she no longer cared about doing the right thing, 'Why am I pushing Ant away to save that arse hole's feelings?' She deleted what she had just written and simply replied,

TO ANTHONY - I'M COMING, JUST GOT A BIT HELD UP. CHRIS ALREADY ON WAY WITH STUART. I WON'T BE LONG X

She rang for a taxi, "Hiya, can I order a taxi to take me to Deansgate, Manchester please, in half an hour, from 51 Hawthorn Close?"

"What name is it?"

"Melissa Morgan," she replied, "the new Melissa Morgan" she followed with quietly as she looked into the mirror.

"That's all booked in love!", the operator said then hung up.

She went over to her dressing table and sat down. She took out a baby wipe and wiped the remains of the smudged and tear-stained makeup from her fiercely blotchy face. Her face stung a little as she wiped a cotton pad of toner over it, and she gently massaged the moisturiser in. Her eyes were slightly swollen from either the number of tears she had cried or the vile way Chris had vigorously forced his thumbs across her eyelids. She looked at her alarm clock; it was worth sparing ten minutes with some ice to reduce the swelling and doing her makeup in 15 minutes rather than trying to cover them in makeup straight away. She raced downstairs and entered the kitchen, which looked a little blurry as the effects of the alcohol began to take their toll. She took some frozen peas out of the freezer, wrapped them in a tea towel and she lay on the couch as she balanced the peas across her eyes.

'Do I really want to do this? I'll just be adding fuel to the fire! What if he becomes more violent when we get home? I know, I'll put my suitcase in the car and if he starts when we get back, I can just run for it and drive off. I might be a bit a bit drunk, but even if I drive around the block and sleep in the car, it will be safer than staying here'; as with every time that she sat/lay 'relaxing' in silence, her anxious mind went into overdrive.

When she thought she had had the peas on for long enough, she dashed back upstairs and started to lug the large suitcase off the bed and dragged it downstairs, 'Why did I do this with my bloody heels on?' she thought. Out of breath, she continued to struggle to drag it to the front door. She threw open the front door, popping on the latch - the last thing she needed was to be locked out. She yanked the great big case down the path to the driveway and threw it up into her boot. She made sure her parcel shelf hadn't been knocked, as she didn't want Chris to know she was poised and ready to escape at any moment. She closes the boot and let out a sigh of relief; at least she knew she had most of her stuff safely away from the house. She had now gotten closer to leaving Chris than she ever had before, as she had only ever played it out in her mind, and she was determined that this time it was going to happen no matter what. She looked up at her house; she had never wanted to leave her house; it was one of the main reasons she had stayed so long. She always hoped Chris would simply return to his mum's. She had painted it and wallpapered it, she was the one who had tried so desperately to make it a lovely home, only for it to end up soulless, no matter how good her interior design skills were. She now realised, though, that her little house was simply bricks and mortar, filled with nothing but painful memories and misery. The numerous scented candles could never completely cover the endless burnt teas and cigarette smoke and she couldn't cover up this side of her life anymore either; enough was enough.

She locked her car and ran back into the house as fast as her heels could carry her as she realised she was quickly running out of time to put on her makeup - which was very much needed at present - as the taxi would soon be here. She redid her makeup just as before and tidied up her hair. Her head was tender from where he'd ripped some of her hair out and she flinched as she brushed over that area of her scalp.

As she went to collect her phone from the bed to pop it in her handbag, she noticed she had 4 missed calls and a text message from Chris.

FROM CHRIS - ANTHONY HAS SAID YOU ARE ON YOUR WAY! A) WHAT THE FUCK ARE YOU PLAYING AT AND B) HOW THE FUCK DOES HE KNOW? WHY R U TEXTING HIM?

'Anthony must have let it slip out and now Chris was going to be even worse with his suspicious mind going into overdrive' she thought, as she began to worry slightly that she was making the wrong decision by going. 'As if tonight can get any worse'. But she needed, now more than ever, to show him that he couldn't keep her down anymore.

BEEP BEEP

There it was the taxi. "Am I really brave... *or stupid* enough to do this?" she questioned herself in her dressing table mirror. She responded by nodding her head reassuringly, grabbed her bag and quickly refilled her hip flask, with the remainder of the wine that was in her glass, and she flew downstairs, shutting the door behind her swiftly so she didn't change her mind.

Melissa entered the club. It was now 10 pm, and everyone had already been out for at least an hour. She felt a mixture of dread and fear, but the other half of her was forcing a boldness within her - it was time to show Chris that she would not be bullied by him any longer!

She couldn't see any of 'their group', so she headed to the bar to get a drink for a bit of extra courage. Although she knew she had probably already had enough at home, she didn't care as she needed as much Dutch courage as possible tonight; she still couldn't quite believe she was standing in the club, especially after what had happened earlier. In the past, she would have remained in tears and shaken, hiding away for days, walking on eggshells around Chris for at least a few weeks after, so she just couldn't quite believe the courage she had found within her tonight. She lit a cigarette as she waited for the barman to get her order and she spun around to scan the room for familiar faces.

"There you go, a double vodka, lime and lemonade for the sexy lady." Melissa turned back around to the bar after realising it was the barman and he was talking to her. She smiled shyly as she handed over her money to pay him, then he winked as he took the money, brushing at her hand in a rather flirtatious manner. She knew he had probably said it to every girl he had served that night but her double serving of Dutch courage and a side order of a nice compliment was just what she needed.

"Melly!", she heard a drunken squeaky voice scream over-excitedly in her direction. She looked over her shoulder to see Louisa stumbling over to her. "I thought you were ill?" she quizzed.

"Yes, I did feel a bit off colour, but I had a little lie down and I felt a bit better. I couldn't miss Stuart's birthday, could I?" she cringed with every word that left her mouth. Even though Louisa had been an out and out bitch with her for years now and there wasn't an ounce of real friendship left, Melissa just felt extremely uncomfortable talking to her at all, knowing what she and Anthony had been up to and the feelings that they shared together. The other week had been bad enough but tonight she felt worse as she knew deep down that she didn't just want to look amazing for herself, but equally, she wanted to bowl Anthony over so that he would take some decisive action with Louisa, instead of the empty promises that he would do it soon.

"Come on, you tart, everyone is over there", she linked arms with Melissa making her feel even more uncomfortable. She also had to ignore her 'tart' remark, something she had flippantly called her on a regular basis ever since Ayia Napa and Melissa was just about reaching breaking point with that, but she had to conserve all her energy for standing up to Chris tonight, so she didn't need another battle on her hands. Louisa was already completely bladdered and was pulling Melissa from side to side as she swayed all the way to the booth where the group of friends were all formed. It was Chris she noticed first; he had a face like thunder, and she couldn't help herself from throwing him a defiant smile and then quickly turning away before he had a chance to react. As she turned away, it was Anthony who she next locked eyes with, who beamed as soon as he saw her, jumping almost instantly from his seat to greet her. The last two weeks had been torturous for her and for him in equal measure, at least she presumed it had been, from the endless unanswered messages that she had received from him, begging her to respond. She tried to remain composed on the outside, but inside she beamed at the sight of him, as much as he did her.

"You look absolutely gorgeous," he whispered in her ear, as he gave her a 'friends' hug and kiss on the cheek. The problem was he may have thought he was whispering, but due to the alcohol he had obviously consumed and the noise level he was competing with in the club, she was sure that Lutfa (their mutual friend) who had just leaned over to hug her, had just heard him - in fact, the look on her face confirmed that she had definitely heard him.

"Hi Lutfa, it's lovely to see you! It's been ages!" Melissa quickly turned her attention away from Anthony and leant over to hug and kiss Lutfa. Lutfa was a lovely, sweet, studious, and quiet girl, who was going out with one of Chris and Stuart's childhood friends.

Melissa continued to hug and greet everyone in the group and when she finally reached Stuart, his concern for her was apparent, as it was written all over his face. "Are you ok now? I hope so, Mel?" There was a sense of guilt in his tone.

"Oh yes, I'm fine, or at least I will be, Stuart. I've got used to feeling like that, but I won't feel like that for much longer." She couldn't help but throw a dig in there and also give a cryptic clue towards her plans to leave him. She knew Chris was watching her like a hawk, trying to read her lips to see what she was saying to people, especially Stuart. She wanted him to feel uneasy, so she was glad that someone had finally witnessed the extent of his appalling behaviour.

As the night went on and the drinks flowed, Melissa avoided Chris as much as possible. He had tried to lay down the law with her again though, by demanding she stop making a fool of him by smoking in front of everyone. He was getting embarrassed by the amount of their friends who kept saying to him that they didn't know she smoked. He also insisted that she had already had too much to drink and that she had better calm down. Her drunken reaction to his demands and incessant moaning was to show him that he was no longer in control of her, so fuelled by her new resolute mindset, she stepped up to the podium in the middle of the club and began dancing seductively. She was fully aware that she would be poking the fire, but she didn't give a damn. In the back of her mind, she was halfway out of the door anyway; she had packed up her things - her life belongings were now compacted into a suitcase and tomorrow she would call Liz and go and stay there for a night or two, but for tonight she wanted to show him that he had not and wouldn't ever destroy her.

Melissa was finding it just as hard to ignore Louisa draping herself all over Anthony, as she was trying to ignore Chris's eagle eyes burning holes in her. Anthony kept looking over with his 'I'm sorry' face when he would have to reciprocate Louisa's affection towards him. So, she lost herself in drink and dance, closing her eyes and entering her own world - nearly stumbling off the podium a few times whilst channelling her inner Brittany Spears. She decided it was time for a toilet break.

As she walked towards the toilets, she felt someone pinch her bum. Ready to slap whichever letch it was, she turned quickly, only to see it was a drunken Anthony smiling like a Cheshire cat at her. She immediately melted, just like she did every time he looked at her like that with his enchanting smile. He leant towards her, sliding his hand around her waist, "I want to kiss you so bad, Liss, you are by far the prettiest girl in this room, and I can't stand being so near to you and not being able to touch you, hold you, kiss you."

She impulsively smiled then her senses kicked in and she saw Chris glaring and Lutfa inquisitively glancing over from the booth in which they were sitting.

"Anthony, people are here - watching! I wish it were different, but it's not and you know exactly how to change that, but you haven't, so unless you want to get a good kicking from Chris - and Louisa for that matter, I suggest you just keep away from me and go back to *your* Louisa."

"Liss, don't be like that, I need to tell you…"

"No, stop, seriously, stop!" Melissa had to turn away, as she couldn't stop herself from melting when she was in front of him, but she was becoming increasingly frustrated by his excuses for why he hadn't ended things with Louisa. She couldn't understand what was stopping him! She thought back to his previous reasons why he hadn't finished things with Louisa and the response of 'Well, you're still with Chris" was now null and void; he knew she had told him she didn't love him anymore - even though she may not have technically left him yet. It would be so easy for Anthony to leave Louisa - he didn't have any official ties with her and although he more or less stayed at her house every night, he wasn't technically living with her, and he did have somewhere else to go, whether he felt at home there or not, so it can't have been that bad? He could at least start spending more nights there to start to show cracks to Louisa and the family, but he wasn't even doing that. He didn't have any legal ties to make the situation messy, so she just didn't understand what was holding him back. She was starting to wonder if she was being played like Liz had been for all these years. Did he really want to leave Louisa? Did he actually have any intention of ending things? From what she had seen tonight and around the dinner table the other week, it certainly didn't look like it, in fact, it looked like he wanted to have his cake and eat it. She marched away from him with her nostrils flared as she headed towards the toilet. Luckily, there wasn't a queue, and she slammed the cubicle door behind her. Just as she locked it, she heard Lutfa calling her.

"Melissa, which toilet are you in?" 'Shit', she thought, here come the questions! She wasn't really prepared to answer anything wisely at this present moment and felt sure she would slip up; she just wasn't cut out for this. She knew that Lutfa had seen her enter the toilets though, so she couldn't ignore her, as she wouldn't usually, so she replied.

"In here", Melissa opened the door, popped her head out of the door and gestured for Lutfa to join her in the cubicle. As soon as the door shut behind her, she began quizzing Melissa, "I know it's none of my business, hun, but what's going on with you and Anthony? He's barely taken his eyes off you all night! His face totally lit up when you first walked over, and I just saw him pinch your bum!"

"Did Chris see?"

"No, he didn't see that, I don't think, well I mean I think you would have known about it if he did! He clenched his fists just from watching Anthony leaning into hug and kiss you when you first walked in. Good job he didn't hear what I did!" Her face turned all concerned-looking as she asked again, "Seriously Mel,I know there's something going on, what is it?"

Melissa looked back at Lutfa; she liked her and felt she could trust her but the shame of saying 'we've been having an affair' made her hold back from telling the truth. "Oh, he just thinks he likes me, but it's not serious, don't worry! It will just be a phase; it will be forgotten about soon!"

251

Lutfa didn't look convinced at all; "Look, I've never thought Chris treated you well enough, hun, you definitely deserve more, so I completely understand if you were tempted, but you're a better person than this..." she hesitated as she held her arm to reinforce her words of advice. "Just don't start an affair hun, please. You will be the one that ends up being the villain - the woman always does, no matter what!"

Melissa felt her heart sink a little; that was exactly why she had just completely played down the whole thing; apart from Liz, Colette and Andie, there was no-one that would understand how she had found herself in this position, no-one that would even really care to listen out of their group of 'friends', not really, because they all had such strong attachments to Chris and his family. She just couldn't bear to have people look at her in that judgemental way again; she felt like they had only just stopped looking at her like that anyway (ever since Louisa spread the 'gossip' from Cyrus - well her version of events anyway). She just couldn't stand the thought of people thinking that she was something that she's not all over again, 'a tart', 'a slapper', 'a slag'. She needed to wrap up this conversation and quickly; she felt extremely uncomfortable, in fact, she realised that she needed to wrap up this whole night and go home. The room was starting to spin, and she feared that if she stayed out any longer it would inevitably end up in disaster, one way or another.

"It's fine, hun, don't worry, it won't get to that. Honestly, I do like him, but I've told him we both need to be single before anything more can happen!" She felt a little less guilty by at least sharing that one half-truth. Her stomach was still churning though, since she liked Lutfa and it didn't feel good lying to her at all. "Anyway, someone might hear us in here!", she said, bringing the conversation to a close by putting her finger to her lips and pointing dramatically beyond the door.

Melissa left the toilets, arm in arm with Lutfa. Anthony was still hovering around the entrance to the toilets and started to make an obvious beeline over to them as soon as he saw them. He was clearly drunk and obviously beginning to care less and less about how things would look to the others in the group. When Melissa spotted him making his way over, she glared at him and tried to subtly shake her head - trying her best to signal for him to stay away. He seemingly took notice as he abruptly stopped in his tracks. Lutfa's eyes swung quickly back and forth between them both after noticing the silent exchanges. Knowing that Lutfa was looking for further signals that things had already gone further than what Melissa had admitted, Melissa smiled awkwardly and directed them towards the bar area.

As they reached some of the others at the bar, Melissa unlinked Lutfa and immediately marched over to Chris, who was standing with Louisa, Stuart, and a few others.

"Right, I'm going to go home. I don't feel well again so I'm going to get a taxi now. Night, everyone!"

There was no hiding the puzzled look on Chris's face. Knowing full well that she had never been unwell in the first place, he felt immediately suspicious. "I'll come with you!" he blurted out after her.

"NO!" she snapped back fiercely. "It's only midnight; you stay here and have fun; I'm just going straight to bed."

"That's what worries me," Chris sarcastically quipped under his breath.

"What the hell's that meant to mean?" Melissa was snarling. The others looked on, watching the exchange and it was clear that not all of them had heard Chris's snipe - nor did they have any inkling as to the real state of their relationship; all except Stuart, who had witnessed the events earlier in the night and now Lutfa, who didn't find it hard putting two and two together. Whilst Melissa snarled and all eyes focused on her, Chris mouthed "who with"; she was unable to contain her anger, and she knew that to Louisa and the others she just looked like she had been possessed by the angry alcohol demon. She knew what they were all thinking, and she refused to start arguing and taking the bait. As usual, Chris had managed to pass insults without being noticed and her emotional responses made her look snappy and unreasonable. There was only Stuart who understood her anger, and his face said it all. She quickly turned on her heels as she shouted, "Have a fab night, everyone!" and headed towards the exit.

"Wait, Mel! You are not going on your own. I wanna make sure that you're ok, Doll." Playing the dutiful boyfriend, she knew Chris was following her as his voice didn't fade. She didn't respond, she just kept on walking, as there was no point arguing.

The taxi ride home was silent, bar two of Chris's digs. "I don't know what's going on with you, but you're up to something", then the second followed swiftly after, "I'm right, I know I am, and I actually think it's something to do with Anthony."

"Oh yeah, as if! Ha! Just shut up, Chris, and leave me alone will you, I am poorly, remember!" she said, trying to divert the conversation away from what he had just stated, but she felt like her whole insides were shaking.

The shoe was most certainly on the other foot at the moment; it was Chris's mind that was tortured with paranoia, uncertainty. It was he who desperately needed answers to his questions, to justify the changes in her behaviour. Part of her enjoyed the fact that he was getting a taste of his own medicine and another part of her just felt continually unnerved by the whole situation. She knew what it was like to be on the receiving end and hadn't wanted to change who she was, to become cruel and deceitful, no matter what Chris had done, just in order to love Anthony. More and more she wanted everything to be out in the open and for them to just deal with the consequences.

When they got home, Chris put the key in the door and opened it, but Melissa pushed past him to get in first - she wasn't going to risk him playing stupid games and locking her outside until he saw fit to let her in. All she wanted was to get into bed, get under the covers and hide away from the inevitable questions from Chris, and from the ones that were crowding her own mind. Throughout the years, an exhausting interrogation scene would almost certainly follow any night out, whether she had been out with Chris or not; the difference was she had never done anything to warrant being interrogated. It was complete mental torture, as he would try and break her down into admitting to things, she was simply not guilty of. This time, any interaction would be justified and now it was a torture of her soul as she didn't recognise the person she had become. All the while, she thought she was growing and it was good for her to have the affair, that it was what she needed to do, but now she realised that she needed to grow for herself, on her own and in tune with who she really was, otherwise she was only sending herself down another path to unhappiness and destruction.

She slung her handbag onto the chocolate brown leather couch, kicked off her heels and proceeded to walk through the lounge into the kitchen; the balls of her feet were burning with each step. She turned on the tap, letting the water run, then she turned and got a glass out of the cupboard. As she filled up the glass, she felt a little uneasy, aware that Chris hadn't uttered a word since they got back. He was still in the living room, but he hadn't turned the TV on. She began to feel like he was just waiting for her to return so he could launch an all-out attack. Her glass was full to the brim with cold water, and she took a gulp as she turned off the tap. Dehydration was beginning to set in, and she wasn't feeling that great. She took a deep breath as she braced herself before walking back through the living room towards the stairs. She didn't even look at Chris; she could feel his presence, and the room was fraught, tense. She waited for the acid tongue attack, even for him to launch for her physically, but he didn't. She tried to get to the stairs as quickly as she could, yet without it looking obvious and without her revealing any whiff of fear. She climbed each stair still waiting for him to erupt, but the house was filled with an eerie silence. Just as she reached the top step the silence was broken,

"I knew it, I knew!" Chris cried out - and it was a cry!

Instinctively, she went to turn and run downstairs, but something in her gut held her back and instead, she clung on to the bannister with one hand, holding her glass in her other hand, with the water spilling over the sides as her hands began shaking. 'He knew what? is this it? is this the moment it all comes out? But how could he know?' Endless questions were pouring into her mind as she waited in anticipation on the top step, waiting to hear anything else before she decided what to do.

"You liar! You are a lying cow!" he blasted loudly through his tears; anger was clearly also very present as well as him being quite obviously upset. She knew she had to go downstairs now, because if she ignored him shouting, it would have looked strange – equally, her stomach was now crippled by the knots that were tightening within her each second that passed and she couldn't just simply hide away upstairs. She had to know what he knew, so she set off hesitantly back downstairs.

When she reached the bottom of the stairs and her foot was firmly planted back into the lounge, she immediately saw Chris, slumped against the wall, crying. He was clasping her phone, staring right at it; her handbag lay abandoned at the side of him. Her heart started thumping loudly and increased in speed; this was it; she knew it was time to face the music. All of a sudden, she didn't feel at all ready to deal with the tsunami of emotions that this would cause for her, Chris, Anthony, Louisa – everyone, and she couldn't breathe at the thought of picking up the pieces in the disastrous aftermath, she was sure they would feel the ripple effects for months if not years afterwards.

Chris turned towards her, and just looked at her with a face full of sadness, as tears streamed down his face. She had never seen him like this, "What, Chris, what's the matter?" he looked more vulnerable and deflated than he had when she told him that she didn't love him anymore.

"THIS!" Chris snapped, his face turning from sadness to anger in a split second as he thrust her phone in her direction. She couldn't see what exactly it was that she was looking at from where she was, only the glare of the green screen shining in the darkened room. She reluctantly moved towards Chris, fearful that his anger may turn to aggression again. It was a text from Anthony; she gulped loudly, her pupils widened, she leant in slightly to read what it said.

FROM ANTHONY - 831

As she read the message her whole body started to relax, she no longer felt scared, simply confused?

"It says 831!" she looked at Chris, her confusion was clearly written all over her face and in her tone,

"I don't get it?" She genuinely didn't understand what Chris would find so upsetting about a few random numbers.

"I saw the way he was looking at you! I saw the spark and I just knew, right there and then, I knew it was him!" Chris was still visibly upset and growing more furious with each word, "I knew I'd lost you, but to him!"

"Chris. what are you…"?

"I'M NOT AN IDIOT, MELLY!" he screamed at her before she could finish. "Just stop! He fucking loves you and if he hasn't already told you that, well, now he has!"

"What? It says 831!"

Again, before she could finish, he jumped in on her sentence, "8 Letters, 3 words, 1 meaning, I love you!"

Melissa could feel her mouth becoming dry and she was speechless. She had no idea what to say or how to respond, so she just stood there trying not to say anything unknowingly through her facial expressions.

"My dad puts it in every card that he sends to my mum." He hung his head as more tears ran down his cheeks.

Melissa remained silent, racking her brain for something to say, but she couldn't think of anything. Her emotions swung from feeling sorry for him to looking at him and feeling completely empty - that he was feeling exactly how he deserved to feel. He gripped at his dark over-gelled hair with hands, throwing back his head and grimacing in frustration, before sinking his head forward again into his hands. Just as Melissa was about to make a move to say something - not that she knew what - he jumped to his feet, still clutching her phone, and grabbing her bag as he got up. His eyes were filled with pure rage. "That bastard," he shouted as he barged past Melissa like she was invisible. He grabbed his car keys off the side table and marched towards the front door.

"Chris, you've been drinking!" Melissa flung herself forward, grabbing onto his arm in an attempt to stop him getting behind the wheel. He never drank very much at all, but she knew for definite he would have been over the limit; that aside, emotionally he wasn't in a fit state to get behind the wheel either. He forcefully shrugged her off his arm, and she stumbled backwards into the arm of the couch. He slammed the front door behind him. The light from the headlights shone into the kitchen, highlighting the shadows within the room. She felt like a shadow herself, a darkened version of herself and she sat dumbfounded by the events of the whole night. She listened as he wheel-spinned and screeched loudly off the drive, sure that it would wake the neighbours and the smell of burning rubber was so strong it seeped into the house. She sat still. She felt empty, ashamed, worried, nervous, scared, lonely and yet slightly relieved; a hundred emotions all rolled into one. She had no idea what would happen next, or what to do next. She wanted to phone Anthony to warn him, as the thought of what Chris would do to him when he saw him made her feel sick, but Chris had taken her phone. She ran over to the house phone and picked up the receiver, but she couldn't dial past 07; she had a complete mental block and she couldn't for the life of her remember his number. She then went to phone Chris, but she put down the handset before she finished dialling his number as she realised there was absolutely nothing that she could to stop him when he was in that frame of mind, plus he was already drunk driving, so she didn't want to distract him further. She had no idea what to do for the best, so she decided to just wait, helplessly, until whatever was about to play out had played out. She glanced at the clock on the DVD player; it was 12.50 pm. She sighed and slumped onto the couch. With the shock of everything that had just happened, she felt surprisingly sober considering how much she had drunk. She threw her head back and stared at the ceiling; she didn't cry, she didn't even feel upset, just completely hollow and numb inside. It wasn't long before she had fallen asleep, the combination of the drink and adrenaline had knocked her out and for a few hours at least, she slept peacefully.

CHAPTER 15.

THE AFTERMATH

The sound of birds tweeting and the sunbeams shining through the window woke Melissa. For a moment, she smiled at the tranquillity of the morning and then everything flooded back to the forefront of her mind and reality hit like a devastating blow to her stomach. She jumped up from the couch and looked at the time; it was 5.10 am. She couldn't believe that she had managed to fall asleep despite the drama of last night. She turned and kneeled on the couch that was positioned under the window in the lounge. She leaned onto the back of the couch as she looked at the drive, through the bushes in the garden to see if Chris's car was there - it wasn't. Her heart raced, 'where is he?'. She presumed it was his intention to find Anthony last night and confront him, but she didn't know for certain. 'If he did go to Anthony, though, why isn't he back? Did he find him? What happened? Has he beaten Anthony to a pulp and now Anthony is in hospital and Chris is in a police cell? What if he never even made it to Anthony because he's crashed his car drink-driving?' Her mind was swirling and becoming increasingly crowded with questions that she couldn't answer. She was becoming more anxious with each scenario that played out in her head, to the point where her conversation lept from her head and she then spoke out loud "Oh my god, what if he's dead!" Her breathing became quite erratic, "STOP! STOP! For Fuck's sake!" she smacked her forehead and shook her head trying to shake out all of the crazy thoughts that were sending her into a blind panic. She spun around from looking out of the window and dashed off the couch towards the kitchen. She went straight for her secret stash of alcohol and grabbed a bottle of wine. She didn't care what time it was; she needed a drink. Again, her crutch of using alcohol to blot out the pain was creeping in, and she longed for the day when she could sort her life out. For now, she simply wasn't strong enough, because at least one of those thoughts that were whirling around her head could be the actual scenario and here she was sat at home with no car keys, no phone, no escape other than by reaching the bottom of that bottle. Whatever today was going to bring, she knew it wasn't going to be pretty and she was in for a long and gruelling day. As she gulped down the wine, her stomach churning slightly as her hangover was just kicking in and lukewarm white wine was hardly the perfect antidote to that, but needs must, it was that or straight vodka and she assumed (rightly) that wine would be the lesser of the two evils at this time of the morning. She desperately wanted to ring someone; she felt as if she would go stir crazy just waiting here, unaware of what had happened, or what was coming next. She desperately tried to remember Liz, Colette's, or Andie's numbers but she had always been particularly rubbish with numbers, and she just couldn't remember any of them, not to mention the fact it would be unfair to ring them at this time in the morning and worry them anyway. This was her mess, her life, and she felt it was unfair of her to disrupt anyone else's lives. The only number she could remember that she knew off by heart was her family home and there was no way she was going to do that.

She just had to wait, either for Chris to return, to get an angry phone call or visit from Louisa or perhaps it would the police that would come knocking, who knew, she certainly didn't and with that, she threw back the remainder of wine that was left in the glass before pouring another.

She paced around the living room, in desperate need of a cigarette, but they were also in her handbag. She regularly took a sip of wine as she wore down the thread of the wool rug in the lounge. She felt completely alone, isolated and trapped in a timeless zone where every minute felt like five minutes and five minutes felt like half an hour. She felt as if she were about to explode. 'This must be what it's like on death row,' she thought to herself rather dramatically as she waited to learn her fate.

It was 11.30 am before Chris finally returned and she hadn't received one phone call or had any other visitors turn up on her doorstep prior to him returning, so she had spent the last few hours going quietly demented and getting decidedly drunk and delving into her ashtray to salvage old cigarette dimps to smoke out of desperation to calm her nerves. She watched as Chris got out of his car and headed up the path from the drive to the front door, trying to find clues from his body language as to what would happen when he came through the door. As he entered the house, calmy shutting the door behind him, Melissa retracted backwards into the timid girlfriend she had been for the last few years and she nervously greeted him, "Are you ok?"

"Yup," he replied swiftly and rather arrogantly. All his upset had seemingly disappeared.

After all the hours she had been waiting, frantically awaiting his return, all she got was 'Yup' and the tone in which he said it stirred a little fire in her belly, and mixed with some wine-induced courage, she found the strength to question his abrupt answer. "YUP? What do you mean - YUP! Where have you been Chris, I've been going out of my mind here?"

"Yeah, I bet you have," he snarled, looking at her in disgust. "Well put it this way, that snake of a boyfriend of yours has wriggled his way out of it, hasn't he! He's fooled every single one of my gullible family, apart from me and Stu. We know he's a lying sack of shit and I WILL find out what's been going on, and that's a promise!"

"Oh!" the word had fallen out of her mouth before she had even realised. She couldn't hide both her surprise and confusion and she realised what she was doing was just cementing the fact Chris had got it right, because just the same as she didn't last night, she wasn't arguing that he was wrong. Her thoughts were more focused on how on earth Anthony had got away with it and what exactly he had said. Snapping out of her thoughts, she thought she best at least attempt to deny it in order to at least try and stop Chris from further making her life a living hell, "Well there you go, you see I told you nothing was going on!" Chris threw another dagger-like glare in her direction, and she wondered why she had even bothered opening her mouth; she was a terrible liar and she wasn't fooling anyone, let alone Chris. She didn't sound in the least bit convincing and the look on his face and the stone wall silence from him said it all. She didn't know what to say next and the drink probably wasn't

271

influencing her choices in the best way, "Why you only just coming back now?" Chris threw another dagger in her direction. "I mean, if it's all sorted what took so long?" she said, trying to sound as normal as possible but coming across as flippant and a little odd.

"I went to my mum's, I waited for them to get back, I hit him, Louisa went mad. My mum and dad woke up. He wriggled his way out of it. My mum wouldn't let me drive home, so she sent me to my old room to sleep. I had to stomach his pretty boy face smirking at me at breakfast this morning as my mum made us 'make friends'. The End"

"But."

"Look, I'm back, OK? So just leave it- now!"

"OK"

"I'm going to the gym!" he grunted, before stomping upstairs, showing he was far from ok. He made a quick change before he came racing back downstairs and shot out of the door without another word. She watched him drive off the drive before collapsing back into the couch, then she took a great big sigh of both confusion and relief, along with a great big swig of wine from the bottle.

She didn't hear from Anthony all day and she didn't dare to contact him. She spent the day watching re-runs of Sex and the City, drinking, smoking, eating chocolate and ice cream. She looked nothing like as glamorous as she had last night; her hair was piled up on top of her head, exposing her tired and strained face, the dark circles, her slightly red bloodshot eyes and her red wine-stained lips. Her pyjamas didn't match and were worn out - just like she was.

Saturday came and went, with Chris absent for most of the day and night and Sunday was pretty much the same. She turned down Sunday dinner with her family, pretending she already had plans; she didn't have the energy to put on a front and she knew they would guess something was wrong. She longed for Monday to arrive so she could speak to Anthony; she so desperately needed to know what exactly happened and what on Earth it was he had said to get out of it? Her previous thoughts that made her doubt his character were playing on a loop in her head, the lies, the times they had nearly got caught, he seemed to be unaffected by any of it; if anything, she felt he thrived on it, and she found it totally unnerving.

Finally, after what seemed like an eternity, Monday arrived. She had never gotten ready so fast; she left for work earlier than normal (for obvious reasons), pretty much as soon as Chris left, and she had waited long enough to ensure he would have left the estate and be well on his way before she dashed out of the door and set off on her way. There was barely any traffic on the roads; it was peaceful, unlike her mind, her head was fuzzy and clouded with a slight headache - a mixture of stress and a hangover following her 48-hour drinking session. She was only 10 minutes from work when her phone started ringing. She leaned over to her handbag, and whilst trying to steady the steering wheel and manage the gears, she delved around her bag desperately trying to locate her phone as quickly as she could. When she pulled it out and glanced at the screen, she felt a wave of relief - it was Anthony.

"Hey, you", he said smoothly,

"Hey!? Oh my god, Ant, it's been the longest weekend ever; I've been going out of my mind - literally! What the hell happened?" before letting him answer she frantically rambled on, "Chris has told me a bit, but it's like getting blood out of stone with him, like it always is. I just didn't know what to say, what to do, I didn't know what you'd said. He said he hit you. Are you ok?" Finally, she paused to catch her breath.

"Yes, I'm fine, well apart from having a right shiner," he chuckled, "don't worry!"

"He gave you a black eye! How did you calm him down?"

"I don't know how I thought of it, or got away with it, but I just played a blinder, acting all surprised, saying 'What you on about? I sent that to Louisa'. He was going completely mental, Louisa and Stuart were holding him back, I thought he was going to kill me!"

"What, that's all you said? There's no way he'd believe or accept that, I know him."

"No, he didn't, but Louisa did. I just said because I was drunk, I must have pressed the second button too many times - you're the second 'M' in my phone and she's the second 'L'. I just said, 'I'm just pissed, I can't even see the screen properly'."

"Yes, but Chris wouldn't have believed that either! Why would you send Louisa a text when you were with her anyway? There's no way that would calm him down!"

For the second time in this conversation (and rather alarmingly), Anthony seemed to find the whole thing rather amusing, laughing as he continued to talk, "That's exactly what he said! I just said I always do romantic things like that, and Louisa jumped in defending me. Then Jackie and Richard came running downstairs, wondering what the hell was going on and you know how much Jackie loves me; well, she was right in there agreeing with Louisa that it was an innocent mistake. I threw in a few crocodile tears, and they sent Chris up to his old room to sleep!"

After everything he'd just been saying sank in (along with his obvious entertainment by it all), her heart sank a little. Chris's own mum had sided with Anthony over her own son, believing his lies, and he thought it was funny that because she loved him so much, she believed him. She had always thought that Anthony was the same as her, a bit of a lost soul, in an unhappy relationship just wanting to find true love and happiness. But seeing his reactions to situations and his behaviour meant that she couldn't help but think he actually wanted and enjoyed the drama, and he actually wasn't like her at all. His hero mask was slipping, and she didn't like what she was seeing. As she thought about Jackie, it actually made her really cross; yes she was more than a little overbearing at times, but she treated Anthony as her own, more or less letting him live under her roof and she began to feel completely appalled by his enjoyment in lying to her.

"It's not funny, Ant! How can you think this is funny? I've been tearing my hair out and you think it's just one big joke! These are people's lives and feelings; it's not funny!", it was the first time she had been furiously cross with him and there was no hiding it.

"I know, I know, I don't think it's funny, it's just a nervous laugh", she knew he was trying to backtrack, and she wasn't buying it. There was an awkward silence for a moment, another first for them, as Melissa had nothing to say to him.

"I thought we'd been busted though, I really did", he continued trying to reiterate he was worried just like she was.

"Well, I still think we have, Ant," she snapped back, "I know Chris and there is no way that he will drop this now, he'll want solid proof and he won't stop until he gets it!"

"Well, we best get looking at these flats quick then, hadn't we?"

"Don't you think we're rushing things, moving in together? We have only been together for two minutes, well, we're not even together right now and we've only been together whilst we've been with other people. I mean it's hardly the best basis for moving in together, is it?" She previously worried about voicing her concerns to him as she didn't want to risk upsetting him or losing him, but she had already officially ended things anyway and she was too mad at him to care right now.

"That's because you don't love me! You have only said it once; I've told you over and over and you never say it!", his tone of voice became completely subdued, and somehow seemed to immediately pull at her heartstrings.

"I do, of course I do, it's not that, I just think we're so young and to just jump out of one serious relationship straight into another is just crazy. I just want to get it right this time, Ant, it doesn't mean I don't…" she hesitated, she just couldn't get those three words out and she didn't know why.

"See, you can't say it! I've told you I'm not leaving Louisa unless we get a flat together. I can't be alone, I need to know you want to be with me, Liss!"

Another red flag: 'I can't be alone'. This whole relationship had been intense from the start but intense with passion, lust, excitement, but now she was starting to feel pressured and a sense of emotional blackmail. That was how it had started with Chris, and she suddenly felt a bit scared.

"Ant, I'm at work now, I've got to go, sorry."

"But you're not due for another 20 mins?" he questioned.

"They asked us all to come in early as someone new is starting. Seriously, I'm sorry but I've gotta go; I'll speak to you later if I can." It was the first time she had ever wanted to get him off the phone and the first time she had ever lied to him. Her heart sank even further.

"OK, well, have a good day, beautiful! Ring me, or text me off Liz's phone when you can."

"Aw, she's not in today so I won't be able to. I'll try and one-bell you though, it's just going to be a bit crazy today with the new starter and stuff," - another lie.

"Oh, ok," he seemed unsure of her behaviour, "hopefully speak to you later then?"

"Yes, speak to you later!" She quickly put down the phone to escape the uncomfortable conversation as quickly as possible.

She was still around 3 minutes away from her work's car park. She reflected on why she had just lied to Anthony about Liz not being in, why she wouldn't be able to speak to him for the rest of the day. She realised that she felt suffocated by Anthony, and she needed a bit of headspace, away from both his and Chris's influences.

CHAPTER 16.

ESCAPE

"Morning, lovely!" said Col, as she peered over the computer and greeted Melissa in the same cheery way she did every morning, before doing a double-take and noticing Melissa's solemn face, "What's up, sweetie pie?"

"Oh nothing, I'm fine." She didn't convince anyone with that statement. Liz had now entered the room and immediately picked up the unusual vibes from Melissa.

"You're fine, are you? Why don't you tell your face that then, kiddo?", Liz gave Melissa a knowing smile, "Come on what's up? This is us you're talking to."

Melissa sighed as she looked at them both before she looked down with her face full of sadness.

"Right, coffee, come on!" Liz announced, turning to Col, "Col come on!" Colette, slightly unwilling, left her station, but Mel was her priority over work, and she could tell she needed to get out of the office in order to talk. Melissa didn't blame Colette for being hesitant in starting the daily schedule with her tales of woe, as this was becoming an all too familiar pattern now, and as much as she knew Liz would happily listen to her dramas all day every day, she was herself growing tired of it taking over everything, including her work. Nevertheless, Colette headed to the meeting book and booked them out for a meeting so that they didn't have to rush back.

"Stay at mine tonight, you need a bit of escapism. We'll have a curry and a few beers, veg out and watch Big Brother."

Mel smiled; this sounded exactly like what she needed, and she did have her suitcase in her car, so she didn't even have to call home for clean clothes and risk arguing with Chris.

"I'd love that, cheers, Liz."

"You can come too, Col, of course!"

"Oh, I'd love to, but Katrina is meant to be coming round tonight for tea." (Katrina was the third person in Colette's marriage; she was supposedly her husband's best friend, but she was certain there was more to it than that, yet she had never found an ounce of evidence to warrant bringing it up.)

"That's so weird! I'm sorry Colette, but it's like why are cooking tea for his mistress?" Liz questioned. Melissa felt terrible; there was Col with her own issues - that she didn't open up anywhere near enough about - and all they seemed to talk about was her, Chris and Anthony!

Melissa was having a lovely night and it was just what the doctor ordered. There was very little boy talk – again, just what she needed - just good Indian food, a few ice-cold lagers to wash it down with and analysing all the people on the reality tv show they had all become hooked on this summer.

Mel's peace was interrupted when her phone started ringing; it was Chris.

"Where are you?" he said very sternly.

"I texted you, I told you, I'm staying at Liz's tonight."

"Stop lying to me, you're with him!"

"With who?"

"You know damn well who! He's not with Louisa, he's playing pool or some bullshit, which means he's with you."

"I take it you're talking about Anthony. Well, you're wrong Chris, I'm sat in my loungewear on Liz's couch. I've had a few drinks so I'm not driving home, so I'm staying here."

"Well, we'll see about that!", then the line went dead.

"What's the psycho want now?" Liz questioned with a dramatic roll of her eyes.

"He doesn't believe I'm here; he thinks I'm with Anthony."

Around 15 minutes later, they were disturbed once again, this time by the sound of loud and frantic beeping that seemed to be coming from right outside Liz's house. It was so loud that they could even hear it in the back room.

"What sort of a dickhead does that at a quarter past nine at night? For God's sake!", Liz jumped off her couch, clearly outraged and she rushed into her front room to investigate. "Mel! Mel!`` followed shortly after.

Mel leapt off the couch to follow her and as she entered the show home-like front room (only used for dinner parties), in the pit of her stomach she knew what was coming before she even joined Liz at the window.

Prizing a gap between the slatted blinds and peering through it outside, Liz was desperately waving Melissa over to join her, "It's Chris, look!" she exclaimed.

"You're joking", Melissa sighed, although that was what she was expecting but she had hoped that it wouldn't have been the case. She joined Liz in looking out of the window, her stomach churning. He was looking right at her, sat in the middle of the road continuously beeping, with several other of the residents of the built-up terrace street now flinging open their curtains to see what all the commotion was. "I best go see him", Mel said. She seemed nervous and like that was the last thing she wanted to do but she couldn't have him bringing this kind of drama to the home of her friend. "Are you sure, honey?" Liz looked concerned, "I'm not sure that's a good idea, he looks pretty crazed, chick."

"He won't go away otherwise", Melissa frowned as she turned to leave the room and head out of the front door. "I'll be watching, just shout if you need me!", Liz shouted after her, keeping her eyes fixed firmly on Chris. Just as Melissa opened the front door, he got out of his car, leaving his door wide open and the engine running, and headed over to her car, which was parked across the street opposite Liz's house, a few doors down. She continued to watch him, puzzled by his bizarre behaviour. He bent down and put his hands on her tyres, then straightened back up and glared at her, before going around the car to do what seemed to be the same thing again. At this point, she shouted over, very aware of the various eyes of the neighbourhood watching the situation unfold, "Chris, what are you doing here?"

"Get in!" he said, not answering her question but simply responding with a blasting demand as he marched back over to his car.

"No! No way, I'm staying here tonight I told you!"

"And I told you to get in!" Soon realising his demands were not going to work, his face changed from demonic to a softer tone as he continued with, "please get in, I won't go anywhere, I just want to talk to you, please, Doll!"

Melissa was so unsure what to do; his increasingly erratic behaviour was making her feel very unsafe around him. Reluctantly, she glanced behind her to catch Liz's eyes still fixated on them, then she turned back to Chris. "OK, you've got one minute, Chris", she tried to hide the quiver of nerves in her voice, "then I'm going back in and you're going home - OK?".

"OK. Thank you", Chris appeared genuinely relieved that she was giving him the courtesy of talking to him.

They got into the car and Chris closed his door, but before they even began talking, a car pulled up behind them.

"Shut your door whilst I just pull over to let this car past."

Something inside made her want to resist the request, but she went against her gut instinct and shut the door anyway. Once her door was closed, he started driving off down the road, "What are you doing, Chris?"

"You're lying to me, you're pretending to be here, but really you're with him somewhere!" the crazed look in his eyes returned and she realised he had played her into getting into the car. He was gathering speed fast as he made his way down the street. "Chris, have you lost your mind? How can I pretend to be here, I'M HERE!"

"You're a liar! Your tyres are warm, so you have been somewhere else!"

"Chris, have you heard how crazy you sound? You've just seen me come out of Liz's! My car hasn't worked since we drove here from work, so my tyres can't be warm!"

"I'm not an idiot, Melissa, you have just driven here now - when I rang you!"

289

He was obviously completely unhinged, and her concerns were growing as he increased his speed.

"Chris, let me out! Let me out now!" She realised there was no point trying to reason with him, as he was convinced his ridiculous notion was the truth and she was scared as to what he would do next. She looked over at him, "I said let me out!" Again, he didn't flinch, he just continued speeding down the street. She started to feel overcome with fear; she had stupidly left her phone at Liz's, but then she never dreamt that he would drive off with her against her will. She felt further unnerved as she recalled just how aggressive and physical, he was towards her the other night. She wasn't prepared to find out how far he would go tonight. They were approaching the long-terraced street, and he would have to now turn left or right onto the main road; she knew he would have to slow down at least a little in order to get out onto the busy road. Deciding she had no choice but to make an exit even if it was a rather risky one, she decided to make a run for it. When they reached the bottom of the street, they were still going at a fair speed, but it was a lot slower than they had been going, so she flung open the passenger door, much to Chris's surprise and she frantically leapt from the car onto the pavement, her body bumping and grazing with each roll. Just as she stopped rolling, she scrambled up from the floor and started running. She only had her slippers on, and the ground was pounding hard on her feet through the soft material. She could feel every stone and crack in the pavement as it pierced through her thin soles. She glanced over her shoulder and saw the driver's door being flung open and Chris getting out. She let out an almighty scream as she feared she would never be able to run away from him, due to his athleticism. She pushed herself harder than she ever had, running with all her might; she daren't look back again in case he was right behind her and the thought of that alone made her scream again. She was completely white now, her eyes terror-stricken and her whole body was pumping with adrenaline. She felt like she was in a horror movie, running for her life. Chris was becoming more and more of a monster, and she was unsure just what he may be capable of. The suspense of not knowing where he was suddenly becoming scarier than knowing if he were right behind her and it made her turn around again. Chris was jogging - not running - not too far behind her and he seemed to be slowing down. Was he lulling her into a false sense of security? She knew he could easily sprint and catch her up; the uncertainty of what he was doing made her feel sick to the pit of her stomach. Then she noticed him keep turning his head back towards his beloved sports car; it seemed like he just couldn't leave it stranded behind. Either way, she wasn't going to slow down, aware that it could be one of his manipulative tricks again. It felt like her energy was dwindling, like she had been running forever, but just as she felt like she couldn't dig any deeper, she caught sight of Liz's car. It was the best thing she had ever seen! Awash with euphoria, she burst out crying as she knew she was near to safety and comfort. Her legs were buckling slightly as her hip pounded from the impact of the fall. Blood was seeping through her lounge pants around her right knee, and she had a searing pain in her shoulder. As she reached Liz's house, the door was already opened, so she flew in, collapsing onto the wooden floor in tears, shaking uncontrollably as she made it over the threshold. Liz was stood at the bottom of the stairs on the phone, "Oh, my god she's here! Mel, what happened? Look at you!" she shrieked, "You need to get here now," she instructed the person on the other end of the phone before putting it down.

She dropped to the floor right beside Melissa and she scooped her up in her arms, in a motherly kind of way and she cradled her head, as Melissa continued to sob. The sight of Melissa all bloody and wounded and the sounds of her cries tugged at Liz's heart and silent tears dropped from her eyes onto Melissa's shoulders.

The warmth of the bath was wrapped around her with the same comfort of a duvet, yet the water stung her grazed body parts at the same time. She lay still and stared at the cuts and bruises dotted around her body. She watched as the water changed colour when the blood dislodged from her skin and pushed to the surface of the water like it was red paint swirling off the brush in the water pot. Her thoughts, like the water, became cloudy; in a zombie-like state, she began flicking the water with her fingers, causing ripples across the water. She thought about the ripple effect of her actions, from that first moment that she replied to Anthony's text. She was tired of replaying draining scenarios, she just wanted to get out of her own head. She pulled towards her the cold glass of white wine that she was cupping with her left hand and rested it onto her head; it was a soothing presence and eased the pressure that was building across her brow. She took a deep breath and rested the back of her head on the bath. She wasn't sure if she had done the right thing letting the police go and give him a warning. She daren't even look at her phone, knowing she would be met with a barrage of abuse and questions from Chris's family. Liz had instructed her to leave it downstairs whilst she had some time out in the bath. The truth was she didn't want time out, as being alone only meant she tormented herself with a jigsaw of thoughts she couldn't ever piece together. She wished that she could just soak away her troubles, but it had gone beyond things being fixed by a nice hot bath.

CHAPTER 17.

DRESSED UP AS LOVE

"Let me go with you, just in case he's there, hun – please?" Liz was clearly concerned; it wasn't just Melissa who had been shaken up by last night's events.

"No, honestly, I'll be fine. You go to work. If we're both off, everyone will think we went on a bender last night! He will be at work, I promise. I'm just going to get the rest of my things and I'll come straight back here if you're sure you don't mind?"

"Mind! Liss, I had no idea what you've been living with, I mean me, and Col knew he was a complete arse, but seriously, hunny, I don't mind in the slightest, quite the opposite, I never want to let you out of my bloody sight!"

Liz reluctantly waved Melissa off, as she drove off in her car back to her own version of a haunted home, full of skeletons in the closet and haunting bad memories.

Once she arrived and she entered her 'home', she felt really uneasy. It seemed colder than it ever had before. It was time to say goodbye to the four walls that had enclosed her for so long; it was time to get some closure from this whole part of her life once and for all. She lay with her eyes shut, so deep in thought, triggered by the lyrics of the song playing in the background. It was as if she was watching herself – watching her spring and summer play out in her head. As she watched the pictures in her mind, she danced her way through the emotions all over again – it had been a never-ending rollercoaster ride of extreme emotions and whatever the outcome, she just had to get off, it was time for it to stop. It was no longer an exhilarating big dipper; it was a never-ending waltzer that was making her feel permanently sick.

As much as he had damaged her, both mentally and physically, she would not be able to live with herself and have peace in her soul by telling him nothing was going on despite both of them knowing that there was – she was a rubbish liar anyway, but she refused to continue these mind games - she was, and must continue to be, better than that. So, she had made her decision; she had to lay her cards on the table. She had known it since she had seen his face after she fumbled her way those through daft excuses that Anthony gave when he read the '831' message that night. She knew she couldn't make him think he was going mad in the same way he had done to her, and last night showed her that that was definitely what was happening - he was now going mad. Any more interrogation and she would have cracked anyway, so she sat up, reached over to her bedside to grab her notebook and pen, and began writing one of the hardest things she would ever have to admit. This felt much more shameful than opening up about the date rape because this had been her own actions made through her own choices. She was a cheat and a liar, and she needed to take 100% responsibility for her actions of late, whatever the consequences.

She scribbled frantically for what felt like hours but was actually just half an hour – there was nothing calculated about the content of the letter, or any attempts of a 'get out of jail free' card thrown in; it was completely from the heart.

Chris,

I know you're not stupid, so for both of our sakes, I cannot keep up this façade any longer. I know that despite you showing it in the worst possible way you do actually love me deep down, but as I said to you last month, I no longer feel the same way about you. Some may say I don't owe you anything – and if your honest with yourself you know I actually don't, but I want to be honest with you, partly to clear my conscious, partly to let you know you're not insane (I know how that feels, you've done it to me for long enough and it's not nice) but partly, well mainly, I'm writing this so that you will let me go. I want you to understand that no matter what you say or what you do from here, it will make no difference at all as to how I feel about you. I actually don't think I have been in love with you for at least a year now and again I think you know this, yet still you cling on.

For the past few months, I have been having an affair, an affair with Anthony. Neither of us meant it to happen but it was just one of those things that just did - that we couldn't stop. I was terribly lonely and unhappy with you, Chris, and although I am not trying to justify my actions to you, I do want you to understand if you would have treated me right then we wouldn't be where we are today.

I know about the girl you were seeing now, the girl that despite the evidence of the phone bills, me seeing her text etc you still used to make me feel crazy – I know the truth now – the difference was it didn't hurt finding out once it was finally confirmed to me. That's when I knew me and you were over for good, and the reason it didn't hurt was because of my feelings for Anthony. I think I love him – and I believe, well he says he loves me too, although we haven't been together for the past two weeks as I knew we couldn't carry on this affair. I have been trying to find the courage for two weeks to tell you, to tell you the truth about Anthony and me – to tell you again that I don't love you so that you actually listen to me, and to tell you I'm leaving you, this house and our lives together for good.

I'm sorry that we have both wasted too much time on a relationship that was over pretty much before it even properly began. Finally, I want/need to tell you that what happened in Cyprus, I wasn't 'asking for it' and I didn't cheat on you or have a threesome behind your back. I was raped; it was date rape, not that any of that would make a difference to 'us' now, but it was just important to me that you knew the truth about what happened, and you can choose to believe what you want as what you think of me no longer matters. As for what happened last night, don't you ever try anything like that ever again or I will press charges, Chris, I am not your property and you need to start realising that, because finally, I have.

Melissa

Her face squirmed as she licked the envelope, the taste of glue only adding to the already bitter taste in her mouth. After sealing the envelope, she had addressed to Chris, she felt a sense of relief and her conscious eased a little.

She glanced around her bedroom; it looked so bare, soulless, yet with or without her stuff there it wasn't, and never truly had been her 'home' however, now it ironically felt as empty as she did whilst she was living here. The only times she didn't feel empty of course were the last few months in which she had spent time with Anthony. As she thought of him, that warm glow radiated from inside and she hoped that soon after the storm blew over, that they would be able to start again - properly this time minus the cloak and dagger. She continued to pack up the last of her things, still unaware as to where she would go on a permanent basis, but this wasn't going to stop her this time, and for now, a few nights at Liz's were a good enough place to start. She was just zipping up her holdall when she heard the key in the front door turn. She glanced at the envelope and gulped; she had not expected him to come home yet - it was hours off when he was due to finish work. She reached out to move the letter off the bed but she hesitated when it dawned on her that he would see all the bags anyway, so she would only have to explain it all, and even with her attempts to regain her strength, she didn't think she would be able to get the words out of her mouth, especially after last night, so she decided to leave the letter where it was. 'Am I really brave (or stupid) enough to do this?' she wondered, but with each step he took upstairs it meant it was too late for her to change her mind. She had absolutely no idea how he would react; would he rage like he did after the 831 text, or would he simply crumble like he did when she told him she didn't love him anymore? She was in unknown territory and her breathing began to increase.

"Stay strong, stay strong, stay strong" she chanted on a loop, quietly to herself, just waiting for him to appear in the bedroom doorway. Then he was there. "Doll, I can't believe you got the police…." he paused, his tone was subdued, and his face became further subdued as he glanced around the room, "What's going on?"

"I, er," as she predicted she couldn't say the words 'I'm leaving'; she just froze. She nervously glanced towards the envelope which inadvertently directed him to it and he walked towards the bed to pick it up.

It was her intention to leave a note on the bed so that when he returned to an empty house it would offer him a clear explanation and it was also to clear her conscious, so that she could escape fully. She wasn't meant to be here when he opened it. She didn't want to watch the devastation and destruction play out in front of her. Yet here he was, home much earlier than expected and reading her note. The opportunity in which she could just slink away had been hampered and so she just stood there watching as he read her words, the full story, warts and all.

He momentarily sank onto the bed whilst reading it; it didn't seem to take him long to read, before then screwing it up into his fist, full of anger. She watched as he went storming out of the room, downstairs and out of the house with an almighty slam to the front door, before screeching his car off the drive. After he left the house, she knew that this time something would definitely happen, it was just a matter of time and she felt like she could literally hear the time bomb ticking, each second nearing a catastrophic explosion. The sound of her heart thumping was echoing in her ears.

"I need to warn Anthony! Shit!" She could only guess that he was going straight to Louisa and to confront Anthony just like last time, but unlike last time though, she didn't have to wait to find out the outcome. But she hadn't had a chance to tell Anthony her plans, about leaving or the letter; she knew he would only talk her out of coming clean and it was something that she had to do. She didn't do it to throw him to the wolves though and she'd had every intention of giving him ample warning. "Oh god, I need to tell him what I've done!" The magnitude of the situation and its repercussions were right here, right now and staring her in the face. She was beginning to regret writing the letter and wondered whether carrying a heavy conscious would have been a better option, but either way, it was too late now, Chris knew the truth and he was on his way to Anthony and Louisa armed with the evidence. Her hand was trembling as she rang Anthony, and each ring seemed longer and more drawn out than the last. "Oh, come on! Please, Ant, answer your fucking phone!" He didn't answer. She pondered as to what she should do - if she rang again, it could arouse suspicion. She then realised that of course that no longer mattered, as the lid was about to be blown off the whole situation; all that mattered now was that Anthony wasn't blindsided by what was about to hit him like a ton of bricks. Still trembling, she started ringing again.

"Oh why, oh why, oh why, for fuck's sake! Answer your phone!" Again, he didn't answer, "AAAAARRRGGGHHHH!" she screamed, as she threw down her phone onto the couch and watched as it bounced off onto the floor.

"Why did I write that stupid letter? Why am I always worrying about doing the right thing? When has Chris ever done the right thing by me? Why did he come home early? We've been here a year and he's only ever come home early like twice!! Oh fuck, fuck, fuck what have I done!"

As she wasn't able to get hold of Anthony, she just waited, praying that he had ended up staying on late at work. She knew Louisa was off on a Tuesday though, and Jackie didn't work at all, so they would both by now be in the know. She wasn't sure why she waited instead of just leaving to go to Liz's as planned. She questioned whether she was some kind of sadomasochist who enjoyed feeling pain. At first, she thought that it was her feelings for Anthony made her stay, but then she thought about leaving, sloping off into the shadows and she just felt that it showed a lack of strength. She was scared, but she didn't want him to know that; all she wanted was to show Chris how strong she was. She knew escaping his clutches wouldn't just be as easy as leaving the house and staying in the next town with her friend, there was no way he would give up that easily, and he had told her as much. Any signs of weakness would make him dig in deeper.

She didn't know what to do with herself, then she thought a good place to start would be to load up the car with all of her stuff while Chris wasn't there, not that she even knew if he would be back at all after reading that letter. She knew that he would have gone straight to his mum and dad's and that by now, she would be public enemy number one, that is if she wasn't already after last night's police visit. Her heart thumped when she thought about Anthony being in the middle of them all, receiving all of the focus of their hurt and anger. She felt guilty - it wasn't supposed to happen this way.

Here it was, the phone call from Louisa; of course, she had two choices - she could answer it or not. Even though it was the last thing she wanted to do, she urged herself to answer it; she wanted to rip the plaster off quickly, just get it over and done with, before the anxiety of finally facing the situation consumed her.

"Hello," Melissa answered, her voice was shaky but completely monotone as she waited to feel the wrath of Louisa's tongue.

"You sad, pathetic slag!"

Melissa bit down on her lip, took a deep breath and closed her eyes.

"You've always been jealous of me!"

"What?!" Melissa had told herself that she was just going to take whatever it was that Louisa had to say to her, regardless of how it made her feel, because she was the 'other woman' and she felt like she deserved it, however, she was so taken aback by her comment - as she had never been jealous of Louisa - that she couldn't help but speak up.

"You! You're a jealous cow! As if Anthony would even look at you, especially as he's with me! You are the most deluded slapper I have ever met!"

And with that, the phone went dead. Melissa was slightly puzzled; it was obvious that Louisa didn't believe what had happened between her and Anthony! Maybe Chris hadn't shown her the letter? Maybe she hadn't spoken to Anthony yet? Maybe he wasn't there - oh how she hoped he wasn't there.

Her phone started ringing again, and this time it was Chris's mum. She pressed the green phone symbol to answer the call but this time she didn't even get a chance to say hello.

"You listen to me, you little trollop, and you listen good! As if it wasn't bad enough you sent the police to my house last night, accusing my boy of all kinds of bullshit and you've broken his heart, that's not enough for you, is it? No, you have to try and wreck my girl's life with your ridiculous lies! You just stay the hell away from my family and me, do you hear me? You are dead to me! I'm completely and utterly disgusted with you!" The line went dead.

"But they're not lies," she said to herself as a lump formed in her throat and it hit her that what Lutfa said would happen, was now happening.

She took some comfort in knowing for definite now that Anthony wasn't there - he couldn't have been. 'Chris must have just told them, and they won't believe it', she thought.

She picked up the phone as tears ran down her face; even though she expected it, their words still cut deep. She dialled Anthony's number, hoping, and praying that this time he would pick up and she could warn him about the complete carnage that had broken out at the Clancy's. The ringing stopped, "Oh, thank god!" Melissa felt a rush of sheer ecstatic relief! Just as she was about to delve into the explosive drama that was unfolding, she was met with a voice, and it wasn't Anthony's.

"You crazy fucking bitch! I've just told you and my mums just told you! Is that not enough? Stay away from me! Stay away from Ant and STAY AWAY FROM ALL OF US!"

Melissa's arm went limp, and she dropped the phone to the floor, muffled screaming and shouting spilled out of the receiver. She felt funny, a little light-headed and her legs felt like they were going to buckle underneath her. Just like the phone had moments earlier, she dropped to the floor herself, her tears had stopped, and her eyes were wide and fixated into space. Without any expression and minimal movement, she reached towards the phone and ceased the call. Not that she could hear anything clearly. She couldn't hear a single word more than she already had; each one had been a crushing blow and confirmation that Anthony had betrayed her.

As it slowly sank in, the tears returned, "he is there." She knew in her heart that he had denied it all and was sat there defending himself, calling her a liar. He knew that she had flushed 'their SIM', that the proof was gone, and it was her word against his. Her stomach ached and she felt queasy - like she had just received a physical blow to her stomach.

The sense of loss was palpable. Her heart sank, she was completely wounded, emotional wounds that she could somehow feel physically. She felt like

310

a fool. She had tried to do the right thing by ending things and being honest so that she and Anthony could stand together and face up to their actions. She didn't want their relationship to be built on the false reality they had been living in so far, an adrenaline-fuelled train wreck without a destination. She had been naive for too long and she realised that their 'together forever 'would not have been forever, but filled with passion-fuelled trysts in the shadows. It didn't mean she wanted to cast her feelings into the darkness, the opposite in fact, but now she questioned everything. The way he looked into her eyes, the words that flowed so freely from his lips, the way they had made love - was it all just lies? He had made her feel like he was her Prince Charming, riding into her life at precisely the right moment, making everything better and loving her the way she deserved. How can it be that it wasn't real, he wasn't for real? She shook her head trying to shake out the memories; she couldn't bear it, and she now didn't know which ones were real and which were not. Tears dripped from the end of her nose as she realised that the man, she had given her heart to was actually someone that didn't exist.

How could he exist? The Anthony that she knew wouldn't have thrown her to the wolves like this, that's when she realised the Anthony, she loved was merely a fictional character, playing to her vulnerability. She felt cheap and foolish as her soft and silent tears turned to heart-wrenching wails. She felt so wounded that it took her breath away. She could feel the lump in her throat start to clutch around it tightly and her tear ducts start to fill without pause, as the realisation of Louisa's statements and accusations hit home. It hurt, it hurt hard. She thought she knew what it felt like to feel heartbroken, but now she knew for definite this was it. Her heart physically ached and the tension building in her head and chest was unbearable. She couldn't accept it- "there must be a reason why he's done this, said these things. Anthony wouldn't do this to me!" Although her words were looking to give him the benefit of the doubt, she continued to sob as deep down, her heart knew the truth.

As the initial shock wore off, the panic set it.

"I need to get out of here!" The need to stay and see how things panned out was no longer necessary, it was now necessary she got out of there. She went white at the thought of Chris returning and his reaction, so she went to grab her phone and her car keys so she could flee before he returned. Whatever wasn't in her car now she was leaving behind. All she wanted, all that mattered was that she got out of there safely. She didn't even glance around to double-check for any of her belongings, she just ran for the door, straight out of it and slammed it shut behind her. The adrenaline helped her push through the pain that was still searing in her hip, and she ran to the car; she struggled to keep her hands from shaking and to put the key in the lock and turn it to get in, using both of her hands in the end to steady them.

She dropped the key into the footwell after struggling again to get the key in the ignition; she bent down to get it and before she lifted her head, she could hear the sound of a roaring exhaust getting nearer. She froze and stared through the windscreen, watching as Chris drove fast up the drive towards her. His face was thunderous, and he slammed on the brakes as their bumpers touched. She gulped both from how close he had come to crashing into her but also from not knowing what would happen next. He stared with eyes like lasers; it was like any minute the hatred that was projecting from them would burn straight through the glass. Then suddenly he swung open his door, sending it crashing into next door's fence panel, then he burst out of the car before slamming it shut again. She quickly pushed down the locks, watching his movements like a hawk. He marched diagonally across the lawn towards the front door, leaving it open behind him; she took that as a signal that he wanted her to come back in the house. She just sat and stared at it, completely unsure of what to do. Did he want to talk, or did he want to hurt her? Would walking back in there be the most stupid thing in the world to do or the best thing she could do to finally break free? It wasn't like she could drive off anywhere now he had blocked her in. So, she took a deep breath, opened her car door, and boldly stepped towards the house. She was unsure as to which side of Chris she would be met with, but as she entered the house, it soon became clear it was his broken side that she would see.

As he sat there sobbing, making her feel guilty, her mind was constantly embroiled in ongoing battles within herself, and it was making her feel sick. Then suddenly the guilt she was feeling quickly switched to a fierce rage; 'why is he so upset pretending he's broken? He broke us! He broke me!' Fuelled by an overwhelming anger and extreme resentment, she could no longer retain her fury; she leapt forward with tears streaming down her face and she repeatedly slapped and punched out at him, "I hate you; I hate you, I hate you!" He cowered, as a build-up of five years' worth of emotions took over her, "I hate you, you bastard, I hate you!" She repeated the phrase like she was possessed, with a mixture of extreme sadness and then it would switch to aggression. He just sat there, letting her, with his hands covering his face until eventually, she collapsed at the side of him, and they both sat silently sobbing and staring into space.

The rain poured down outside; it was as if the sky had saved up all the tears she had cried inside over the years, and they had finally been released. She had several missed calls from an obviously concerned Liz, so she nipped outside for a cigarette and phoned her at the same time. Melissa explained everything that had happened, along with

315

the fact that she was unable to go anywhere just yet as her car was blocked in.

"I'll come and get you!" Liz offered, desperately wanting Melissa out of that situation.

Melissa took a sharp drag on her cigarette before replying, "No, honestly, don't worry. I want to leave with all my stuff. I'm totally drained; it's been the worst day, but I'm not scared, he's just devastated actually, he's not angry, in fact, he's barely saying a word. If I have to wait until morning, I will just stay in the spare room; there is no way he will miss work so I will wait until then."

"Oh Mel, are you sure? I am worried about you; the guy is insane!"

"Liz, honestly, I will ring you or the police if I get scared about anything but when I leave, I want to leave and not look back. I don't want to have to come back here ever again."

"Ok, hunny, well you know where I am, ok?"

"Yes, and thanks, Liz, I really appreciate it."

"Don't mention it, hun. Just take care of yourself, please?"

CHAPTER 18.

A STEP TOO FAR

Melissa blinked several times and brushed her legs underneath the cotton covers as she stirred. The room was darkened but not completely, as the first light of a summer's day crept through the cracks in the curtains. She had been too tired to close them properly earlier, before she collapsed onto the spare room bed and she turned away from them, facing the wall. As she rolled over, a figure sitting at the end bed startled her and her heart began to race. It was Chris, sitting in statuesque nature, just staring right towards her.

"Chris! For God's sake, are you trying to give me a heart attack? What are you doing in here?"

She was unnerved by his presence and the motive behind him sitting there.

"I just wanted to watch you sleep."

"Chris, you shouldn't be in here! We are not together anymore. This my space and you're invading it! Watching me sleep, Chris, it's not right, will you just go, please!"

"I don't want to," he shuffled further up the bed towards her.

Her heart rate flared again, and she moved up the bed herself, backing up towards the headboard. "Well, I want you to! Chris, I mean it, can you go please?" she hoped that by staying polite towards him he would respect her wishes - he didn't. He moved up the bed again and put his hand under the covers reaching out towards her leg.

"Get off me!" His aura filled her with fear and a sense of panic. He didn't move his hand, despite her moving her legs away. She pulled her knees up towards her chest and clasped then together tightly with her shaking arms wrapped around them.

"Doll, please, I just want one last time with you."

"Chris, I've asked you nicely and now I'm getting pissed off. Leave this bedroom right now or else I'll call the police!" He laughed off her threat as if it would either never happen or that it didn't bother him, she wasn't sure which, but either way, she knew the police route was not getting him out of there; "And your mum," she continued.

With the mention of his mum, his whole disposition changed, the sinister look in his eyes faded and he looked down. As his eyes dropped down, he lifted his body off the bed using his arms, his body language seemingly deflated, he walked silently out of the door closing it behind him.

Melissa let out a huge sigh of relief along with a few tears; for a moment she felt he was going to force himself upon her and she wouldn't have been strong enough to fight him off. It was right there that she knew that as soon as he left for work, she had to go straight away.

FOUR DAYS LATER

In a moment of pure weakness, she texted Anthony. She knew it was risky, but in that moment, she just wanted him to hold her in his arms, the way he had when she told him about Ayia Napa and make her feel like everything would be ok. she just wanted to talk to him, even just to get closure.

TO ANTHONY - I KNOW WE CAN'T GO BACK TO WHERE WE WERE. I KNOW YOU FEEL LIKE I LET YOU DOWN BUT PLEASE DO ME ONE THING? PLEASE LISTEN TO WHITE FLAG BY DIDO ESPECIALLY THE LAST LINE. IT'S EVERYTHING I WANT TO BE ABLE TO TELL YOU IF ONLY WE COULD TALK. X

As soon as she had sent the text, she burst into tears. She felt like she had skyrocketed back in time by 3 months and had returned to the pathetic, needy, lonely young girl that had started out in the treacherous waters of an affair in the first place, that girl even she didn't recognise as herself, that she thought she had managed to leave behind - how could she be back here? 'How could everything be such a mess? How had it all fallen apart like this?' her thoughts were tormenting her once again. She felt so sure that Anthony did genuinely love her and that he was bound to come round at some point, that he would tell her that he just got scared to admit it in front of everyone and that he did love her, but with each day that certainly slipped away. She felt so annoyed at herself for spoiling it all; why had she pushed away such a good man? 'Why didn't I just look at the flats with him? I could have been happy now, not alone', she continued to sob.

She feared she may never escape Chris's clutches, especially after his recent unnerving behaviour with the car and in the spare room the other night. He was constantly bombarding her with texts and phone calls, although she hadn't answered any of them. He just kept reiterating that he was able to change and that he wasn't going to let her go. He painted a wonderful picture of the future that they would have together and even started discussing a wedding and children. She may have felt terribly alone, she had hit rock bottom and she felt that she had nowhere to turn, but there was no way she was falling for the same old patter he had always given her whenever she gave him even the slightest inkling that she had had enough. Beyond that though, all she felt for Chris now was pity and resentment - although she did try and battle against those feelings. There was no way she would ever go back with Chris now just because she was frightened of the unknown and being alone. As she thought about how many years she had wasted on this toxic relationship, she mourned for the years of her youth that she had lost. She felt saddened by the fact that she was stripped of her dignity in Ayia Napa and then further allowed a different man to stop her piecing it back together and stripping her dignity away even further. She didn't want to beat herself up any longer; she couldn't change the past, but she could no longer be ruled by all of these demons.

As she sat reflecting, trying to pull herself out of this black hole that she had found herself in, she heard her phone beep, and her heart skipped and the flutters she had so missed in her stomach returned as she smiled to herself and said aloud, shedding a happy tear, "he's replied!" She reached out for the phone and her smile quickly faded as she studied the screen,

FROM LOUISA - YOU SAD PATHETIC COW. ANT HAS JUST SHOWED ME YOUR MESSAGE AND WE LAUGHED OUR HEADS OFF. WHEN

WILL YOU GET IT INTO YOUR HEAD, THAT YOUR LITTLE LOVE AFFAIR WAS ALL IN YOUR TWISTED MIND. HE FELT SORRY FOR YOU SHOWED YOU A BIT SYMPATHY AND YOU JUST COULDN'T STOP THROWING YOURSELF AT HIM. GET YOUR OWN MAN YOU SLAG AND DO US ALL A FAVOUR AND STAY AWAY FROM US ALL!!!

She felt like she had just been tasered, utterly stunned and numb from Louisa's text. The message completely floored her, and she felt that she had to read it all again in order to properly compute it and the entirety of its contents. After digesting the message, she felt utterly ripped in two by Anthony's betrayal and the humiliation of the message.

This week had already been so hard, and she felt the weakest she had in a long time. She felt so angry and hurt by Anthony's betrayal, yet she was still heart-achingly in love with him, and she just couldn't seem to switch it off. She had had zero contact from any of their joint friends and she knew what they were all thinking, as they had only heard Anthony and Louisa's warped version of events. Such events had been spread with the underlying message that she had gone after Louisa's man and had concocted vicious lies after he rebuffed her continued advances.

Liz and Colette had gone away three days earlier and it couldn't have been more ill-timed. Of course, that wasn't their fault and it had been booked 18 months ago before Melissa had even started working there. She hadn't even thought about joining them, even though they encouraged her to; she wouldn't dream of gatecrashing their holiday with the amount of baggage she was carrying around at the minute. Liz had left her key with her and insisted that she continued to stay there even whilst she was away. Although she would have previously felt cheeky taking her up on the offer of staying there whilst she was away, after Chris's behaviour the other night, there was nowhere else she would rather be, well, apart from at home surrounded by her family. Her family were clueless as to what she was enduring emotionally. She felt ashamed of so many things and felt too much of a failure to let them in to help her. She didn't want them to know anything until she felt stronger and able to answer the questions they would inevitably ask without falling apart. She wanted to be back in control, or at least be able to act like she was before she opened up to them. She knew it would hurt them too much to see her so low and fragile and she didn't want to be the cause of any pain for them. The only problem was that at this moment she had no idea how she would ever feel in control or put a front on ever again.

She had phoned in sick again today, as she couldn't face going to work, and she was also afraid Chris would turn up there, as she had now stopped all communication with him. Right now, he had no idea where she was, and she wanted to keep it that way. She was so worried that he would come by Liz's house to find her, that after unloading all of her belongings into Liz's spare room, she drove all the way to the train station, parked up and Liz drove them back to her house before she left for her holidays in order for him to just keep on driving by if he should pass.

Despite it only being 12 o'clock, she opened a bottle of wine - after that message from Louisa, she needed it. She turned on the radio and began drowning her sorrows. After receiving that brutal text, she now felt worse than ever and after polishing off the full bottle of red within half an hour, she searched for something to drink at Liz's - which wasn't hard. As she only found spirits and didn't have any mixers, she decided that straight Peach Schnapps was the safest option and the only one that she could stomach straight. She felt so hollow and empty inside. She felt cheap all over again, just like she had in Cyprus, and she hated the thought that Anthony had just dressed up his feelings as love, when all he really wanted was to get her into bed and like an idiot, she had fallen for it. The more she sat there alone, the more she felt a new level of loneliness and she started to cry. She so desperately wanted to have someone just tell her that they loved her, but she couldn't bring herself to reach out to the handful of people that she knew did. Her silent sobs turned into harrowing wails. Then a thought that had never yet even entered her head suddenly was whirring around like it was the only answer. What if I just ended it all? What if I wasn't here anymore? I can't stand this pain, this loneliness anymore and everyone would be better off without me anyway. The more she thought of it, the more she cried, but in her drunken and low state, it also seemed like a feasible option. She got up off the couch and stumbled into the kitchen, opening random cupboards looking for Liz's medicine cupboard. There they were packets of tablets staring right at her. Paracetamol, Cold and Flu, some out-of-date hayfever tablets, Rennie's and some with a name she was unable to read let alone pronounce. She concluded they must have been given to Liz for her back pain, so she removed the packet along with the Paracetamol, crying as she slumped to the floor on the cold kitchen tiles and emptying out a couple of Paracetamol, started to swig them down with the schnapps. They didn't go down easy, and she was throwing her head back and forward trying to get them down - and they were only the first two. She then took two of the back pain tablets, followed by two further Paracetamol tablets. She looked over at the wall, where Liz had a display of photos including some of herself, Liz and Colette, and it suddenly made her realise they had had so much fun together; she hadn't always been a drain on them; she glanced at the other pictures, and it was Liz with her family. Her thoughts turned to her own family and just how devastated they would be if she took such drastic action when they weren't even aware that she was so near the edge in the first place. The thoughts of her family, how low she was and the realisation of what she was in the middle of doing, made her feel physically sick, right to the pit of her stomach. A picture in her mind of her dad crying beside her graveside made her instantly heave. In quick succession another vivid image flashed across her mind, this time it was her little sisters though, standing side by side, arm in arm, tears streaming, asking her why over and over. She heaved again; this time she didn't try to hold back, she didn't want to stop the wave from making her actually be sick, she wanted to be sick. She hurriedly got up from the floor and steadied herself by clutching onto the marble worktop. She pushed the washing-up bowl within the sink to one side as much as possible, trying to force a gap which she could be sick in. As she was sick, her tears increased, as did the realisation of how close she was to making the biggest, most stupid mistake of her life that she could ever make, and the main reason running through the core of why she had found herself there was because of men. She wanted to make sure her stomach was completely clear of any drink and any medication. She'd had an epiphany and it was time to sort herself and her life out for good. She stumbled back into the lounge to try and locate her handbag. Once she found it, she rummaged around each and every section of it until she came across a tatty business card for a counsellor that Liz had given her a while ago. After dismissing it once before, she knew now it was exactly what she needed.

She had become so enthralled by the idea of living within a love story that she had been blinded by the red flags – they say love is blind and she was a living cliché.

CHAPTER 19.

THE FINAL CHAPTER

The counsellor had made her realise that she wasn't necessarily in love with Anthony, she was in love with how he made her feel, because she wasn't able to make herself feel that way. He had made her feel alive, awake, confident, and free, yet as soon as their relationship ended those feelings ended. She helped her to see that unless she learned to love and respect herself, then she would continually rely on a man to make her feel that way and she would always be vulnerable and she would most probably live her life in the same vicious circle, getting into relationships with the same kind of man repeatedly.

Chapter 18. The Final Chapter

It had taken her six weeks of going to see the counsellor twice a week, but she was finally stitching her broken soul back together. She still had a long way to go to find herself and love herself again, but she was on the right path, she just had to learn how to stay on it now.

She had spent the last six weeks staying at different friends' houses, including Andie's and Colette's and intermittently with her family, so she didn't impose on Liz too much, even though Liz insisted that she would be doing no such thing and she loved her staying with her.

After Chris's efforts to contact her intensified to the point where he was more like a stalker, popping up wherever she went, Colette arranged for her solicitor friend to send a warning letter to Chris to state that if he continued to harass her then he would end up with a restraining order - it seemed to be working for now.

She had confided in her family that her relationship was over and had stayed at home for as many nights as she could bear Linda, and as many nights as Linda could bear her without kicking off with Pete and making her dad's life a misery. Even though she was living her life out of a suitcase, week by week she felt that even though she had no real direction, she was heading the right way somehow.

It was only when Vicki called her last week to say that a friend of hers had a room becoming available in a house-share in London that Melissa decided that a big move was exactly what she needed. She took the call as fate and she agreed to let the room and take the plunge, despite the fact she had never even met her fellow housemates. She didn't even have a job lined up, but she knew if she had managed to get through the last few years and come out in one piece – well, just about - then she could get through anything.

Despite knowing that their love wasn't real, she still had moments where she longed for Anthony to ring her, although it was more for closure than anything, not knowing what was the truth from their time together and what was lies in the whole situation was the hardest thing to deal with.

Through solicitors, Chris had agreed to buy Melissa out of the house and even though it was for way less than what she should have had from the house, she agreed to the amount just get it over with as quickly and as painlessly as possible and finally close the door on that chapter of her life. In just another 5 weeks, the money should be transferred, and she would no longer have any association with Chris Clancy or any of his family. She had received a few messages from Stuart, who wanted to let her know that he didn't blame her for any of it and that he wished her well. He stated that he wished that they could remain friends but for obvious reasons they couldn't. Melissa knew that he saw Chris's behaviour that night when he came to pick them up and she appreciated him reaching out to her, he was the only one who had, apart from Lutfa who was also concerned for Melissa's wellbeing and how she was doing now that everyone had turned on her, just like she'd predicted.

It was as she left her last counselling session that she remembered something her Nana used to say, 'Sometimes things have to fall apart in order for things to get put back together the right way.' It really struck a chord with her; even if Chris hadn't been so abusive, he wasn't the man for her. Even if Anthony hadn't been such a coward underneath his white knight costume, he wasn't the man for her either. Everything had fallen apart because it was meant to, it had to, in order for her to live the life that she deserved.

She slammed the car door behind her; her whole life was packed up – two suitcases and 3 boxes. As a tear graced her cheek she smiled, it was a tear of pure relief. Both Liz and Colette had helped her clear out of Liz's spare room, where she had been storing her stuff whilst she sorted her life out. They were both teary too as they embraced her.

"You take care, hunny, I'm proud of you! We'll be down in London soon to shake our booty's with you, so don't think that you are getting away from us that easy!" Liz smiled, blinking away her tears as she gave Melissa the biggest squeeze she could.

"You drive safely, lovely, we're really going to miss you! Especially at work!" They all laughed at the fact Colette brought up work during their goodbye's.

She had said her goodbyes to her family earlier as she feared if she set off from there then she wouldn't stop crying all the way to London.

Melissa got in the car and wound down the window, "Thank you both so much, you have helped me more than you'll ever know, love you both," her voice broke as she tried to fight back the tears. She felt like she was leaving behind the two big sisters that she never had. She would never ever forget what they had done for her.

"Go on, get going before I ruin my mascara completely!" Liz joked.

She had no idea what kind of life awaited her, or if she was truly ready to embark on a new life in London, but one thing she knew for certain was that it was bound to be better than the one she was leaving behind. She firmly wiped her cheek, feeling happy and determined, as well as a little scared. She put her keys in the ignition and turned them to start the engine. The radio blasted out, and as she set off, she looked in the rear-view mirror as Liz and Colette waved her off frantically. She put her foot on the accelerator; 'don't look back now' she reassured herself. She had no real plan other than for the next few days, but for now, that was all she needed. As she left the side street and turned onto the main road, she felt liberated and free, not to mention proud, proud to have found the strength to break free of the chains she had thought were ironclad for so long; she was ready to finish this chapter of her life and she was ready to start afresh. She was filled to the brim with fear, but equally with an insatiable curiosity to see more of the world and make the most of her life, and so she kept driving and didn't look back.

Help and support

If you feel affected by issues raised in this book, there is help and support available.

Asking for help and leaving an abusive relationship is often not easy for a number of reasons, especially if you are fearful of what your partner might do or if you feel isolated and unsure what to do. Your self-confidence may be low because of the impact of the abuse, and this can make reaching out seem overwhelming.

Domestic abuse can take many forms including emotional, sexual and financial abuse as well as physical abuse. You do not have to be hit to be abused. Power and control is at the heart of domestic abuse, and in 2015 coercive control became illegal in England and Wales, which means that it is illegal to use coercive and controlling behaviour in a relationship. Abuse can include being isolated from friends, family and other support, being cut off from support networks and having your day-to-day activities monitored and restricting your access to your money and resources. You may feel like you are never able to relax because you are worried how your partner will react.

Women's Aid is the national domestic abuse charity providing support for women and children, and there are many ways you can seek information, help and support for you, or a friend. Got to www.womensaid.org.uk for the Women's Aid Live Chat service (open daily 10am-6pm), the Survivors' Forum, The Survivor's Handbook, which includes information on safety planning, and the Domestic Abuse Directory with details for your local domestic abuse service. There are also links for national domestic abuse helplines in the UK including services for men and the LGBT community.

Women's Aid: @womens_aid

THE BRAND-NEW BOOK BY LOLO STUBBS:

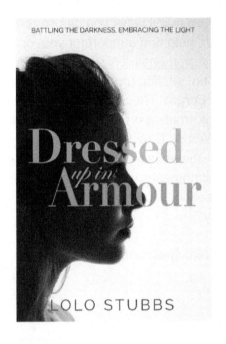

www.dressedupinarmour.com/

LOLO STUBBS

www.lolostubbs.com/

LOLO STUBBS

Join the conversation and
share your reviews:

 @Lolostubbs.author

 /Lolostubbs.author

 @Loloauthor

 Dressedupaslove.com

 Lolostubbs.com

We'd love to hear from you...

Printed in Great Britain
by Amazon